CLEO PORTER
AND THE
BODY ELECTRIC

CLEO PORTER

AND THE

BODY ELECTRIC

JAKE BURT

FEIWEL AND FRIENDS
NEW YORK

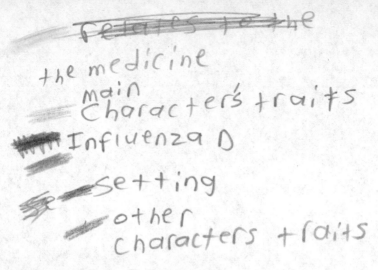

~~relates to the~~

the medicine
main
Character's traits
Influenza D
setting
other
characters traits

A Feiwel and Friends Book

An Imprint of Macmillan Publishing Group, LLC
120 Broadway, New York, NY 10271

Our books may be purchased in bulk for promotional, educational, or business use.
Please contact your local bookseller or the Macmillan Corporate and Premium Sales
Department at (800) 221-7945 ext. 5442 or by email at
MacmillanSpecialMarkets@macmillan.com.

Library of Congress Cataloging-in-Publication Data is available.
ISBN 978-1-250-23655-5 (hardcover) / ISBN 978-1-250-23656-2 (ebook)

Book design by Mike Burroughs
Feiwel and Friends logo designed by Filomena Tuosto

First Edition, 2020

10 9 8 7 6 5 4 3 2 1

mackids.com

For Josh and Jon

plot
_____

1. gets the medicine

CHAPTER ONE

Three objects sat upon the carpet in Cleo Porter's living room: an apple core, a human skull, and a package wrapped in red.

It was the last of these that had Cleo well and thoroughly vexed. She lay on her stomach, bare feet waving in the air behind her and chin digging into the back of her hand. Her belly was starting to get itchy from the carpet fibers poking through her shirt, but she just wriggled a bit to scratch it. She'd stare at the glossy box for another hour if she had to, until it either disappeared or made sense.

First there was its color: deep red. Blood red. "Hemoglobin red," as Cleo would say. Of course, she knew what it meant: the package contained medicine. But she wasn't sick. Her mom wasn't sick. Her dad wasn't sick. And Ms. VAIN? Well, she *couldn't* get sick, so there was no reason Cleo could see for them to have medicine.

Then there was the label:

MIRIAM WENDEMORE-ADISA

412263

25 MAY 2096

The address was right. Cleo had even sung the silly little song her dad had taught her to remember it ("The number starts with four-one-two: a place to live for me and you! Round it off with two-six-three: safe from influenza D!").

The date was obviously right.

The name?

That was all wrong.

Cleo pulled up to her knees, dug her nails into her belly for a few satisfying seconds, and then reached for her scroll. When she had it unfurled, it clicked into a stiff board, and she propped it against the package. A simple touch in the middle brought the screen to life, and an array of pillowy blue letters appeared:

Virtual Adaptive Instructional Network
Use Voice Recognition to Log On

"Head, shoulders, knees, and toes," Cleo said quickly. The pudgy letters dissolved instantly, replaced by the fretful face of her teacher, who peered at Cleo over her bifocals.

"You've been gone for a good deal more than 'a few minutes,' Cleo," Ms. VAIN observed.

Cleo glanced at the icon behind Ms. VAIN's right

shoulder. The screen zoomed in, replacing the matronly teacher's face with that of a clock.

"It's only been seventeen," Cleo retorted, rolling her eyes. "I can take a little break. The test isn't until next week."

Ms. VAIN seized the opportunity to reclaim the screen. "Seventeen minutes is more than enough time to eat an apple. Besides, your test is in five days, darling. Five."

"And I've been studying for it since I was six. That's half my life!"

Ms. VAIN wagged a virtual finger at her. "Some have been at it longer than that. Now, where's your skull? We were reviewing the names of the sutures ..."

Cleo grabbed the skull and held it in front of her scroll. "Metopic, coronal, sagittal, lambdoid. There. Now can I ask you a question?"

"Always and anything, love."

"Who is Miriam Wendemore-Adisa?"

Cleo repeated the last name letter-by-letter, just to be sure.

Ms. VAIN blinked—something she did only when consulting the database. Then she shook her head. "Sorry, Cleo. I don't have information on anyone by that name. I could expand my search to fictional characters and variant spellings, if you like?"

Cleo frowned. "No, thank you. It's not a historical figure or anyone like that, anyway."

"Someone contemporary? Ah. Sorry there, love. VAINs don't have access to the directory. Why do you ask?"

Cleo picked up the scroll and turned it around, letting Ms. VAIN see the package.

"That's where I got the name."

Ms. VAIN wore a reassuring smile as Cleo flipped her back. "It's probably for one of your mother's patients, yes?"

Cleo squinted skeptically at the package. "I don't know. I mean, it's not like my mom can just give her the medicine. It's no good *here*."

"Best ask her when she's done with work, then. In the meantime, may I suggest a thorough review of the optic nerve?"

A slowly rotating image of an eyeball replaced Ms. VAIN's patient face. Cleo's eyes weren't on it, though. Instead, she was staring at the door that led into her mother's office. The seal around the edge pulsed a quiet orange. Her mom was in surgery.

So that was a dead end, then.

"Maybe our tube malfunctioned?" Cleo said suddenly, and she scrambled to her feet. Ms. VAIN's voice followed her.

"Tubes don't malfunction, dearie! They're just tubes. And packages don't get delivered to the wrong place."

Cleo ignored her.

The tube jutted into their kitchen like a giant made of glass had shoved its finger through their wall. Cleo and her father had used paints to decorate it like a garden box, and every time a delivery whooshed in, it looked like the flowers and butterflies and bees were alive with light, if only for a second. When she was younger, she'd press her face to the rounded end, watching for deliveries and screaming ecstatically every time the shutter in the wall opened. That was her dad's cue to slide open the top of the tube and grab the delivery, whether it was food or soap or a replacement scroll.

Cleo peered through the glass the same way now, but Ms. VAIN was right.

It was just a tube. Their tube. It wasn't broken, and it certainly wasn't capable of magically manufacturing medicine.

Still, *something* weird had happened, and it involved that tube. Cleo knew it.

Mostly because, other than the tiny air vents and the compost chute, it was the only way anything got into or out of their apartment.

Ever.

CHAPTER TWO

O ne day, right after Cleo had turned three, her mother discovered her in her room performing surgery on Elly the Elephant. She had her wild cloud of brown curls tied back as best her little fingers could manage, and she wore a pair of her own underwear over her face like a surgical mask, her serious gray eyes peering through the leg holes. Once they had cleaned up the stuffing and sewn Elly back good as new, Knowles Porter asked her daughter just what exactly she thought she was doing.

In a tiny, wise voice, with every word perfectly pronounced, Cleo replied, "Emergency appendectomy, Dr. Porter. Nothing else for it." smart, creative.

Cleo's mom decided, then and there, that her daughter would follow in her footsteps as a drone surgeon, even though it meant Cleo would have to start on the medical instruction track by age six, and even though it meant her daughter would face what, by all accounts, was the most rigorous, high-stakes, cold-sweat-and-nightmare-inducing gateway test of any profession, anywhere. To her infinite credit, Cleo dove right in: her new favorite toy became a life-size model of the human skeleton, she could name all the bones of the inner ear by age four, and she could regularly be found tearing through the apartment like a little bug-eyed Frankenstein, her mother's huge drone goggles covering half her head as she scurried to find the cure for whatever fatal illness her father was feigning at the time.

On her sixth birthday, Cleo had received her prized possession: her scroll. Ms. VAIN was greatly appreciated by child and parents alike; she answered all of Cleo's questions, which allowed Bowman and Knowles Porter to take a much-needed break from doing the same. And one of the first questions she had asked?

"Where is everyone else?"

"Everyone else, love?" Ms. VAIN had replied.

"Not like Mommy and Daddy. I know where they are. But the people on the screens. The people in my games. The other kids you're helping. People like that."

Ms. VAIN blinked several times. Then she cheerfully asked, "Would you like that information in a timeline, an encyclopedia entry, a documentary film, or a story?"

"Story, please. Always story."

"As you like. Comfy, love?"

The little girl held up a finger, then ran to get her silky blanket and the skull from her model. She set her scroll up stiff, positioned the skull so it too could see, and popped her thumb in her mouth.

"Mind the sucking, Cleo," Ms. VAIN chirped gently. "Remember what we—"

"Oh, yes. Malocclusion of the central and lateral incisors. Right. I'm still working on it."

"I know, love."

Cleo wiped her thumb on the blanket and drew in her cheeks to make fish lips instead. Ms. VAIN began.

"Everyone lives in apartments, just like you do, Cleo. It keeps them safe."

"From what?"

"These days? Not a great deal. At least, nothing that has been recorded in the database. But it wasn't always that way."

"Influenza D?"

"Just so. And that's where this story begins. The year was 2027, and doctors—"

"Like Mommy?"

Ms. VAIN nodded, folding her hands atop her desk. "Sort of like your mother, yes. They discovered that many people, all around the world, were getting very sick, all at about the same time."

"Did they die?"

Ms. VAIN slipped her bifocals up to sit along the peak of her peppery white hair. It made her look even kinder than usual.

"Yes, Cleo. Many, many did die. And if this is too

upsetting, we can play a game instead. I know a delightful dance that helps with the names of the joints."

Cleo's wispy eyebrows knotted, and she shook her head. "No. More story, please." *brave*

Ms. VAIN waited until Cleo had gathered up the silky blanket and wrapped herself in it. Then she continued.

"Most of the world got sick, and the doctors couldn't help them. Just as bad, they couldn't figure out what was wrong. Everyone seemed to be ill with different things— just at the same time. And because the doctors, scientists, and politicians couldn't agree on what was causing the malady, they didn't find a cure."

"Not ever?"

"Not ever, no. In fact, it wasn't until ten years later that they even discovered what it was: a strain of the flu that changed constantly. It started in livestock, like pigs and cows. Then it spread to humans. The *D* used to simply denote the strain of flu, but it came to stand for the Greek letter delta, which means 'change.' Every time it got passed from one person to another, it altered slightly. We call this 'mutation.'"

"So there was no medicine."

Ms. VAIN shook her head. "None. And by that time, so many had passed—"

"Does 'passed' mean died?"

"Yes, love. They're synonyms. So many had died that everyone who was left decided a drastic solution was necessary. They built great structures to protect the remaining healthy people. Those people would be kept separate from each other, each family closed in their own apartment, just in case. And because they were separate, influenza D couldn't spread. It was a desperate gamble, but it worked. The last recorded case of the flu was in 2043, and no outbreak has ever occurred within one of the buildings."

"What about outside?"

Ms. VAIN blinked. "I have no data on that. But the very good news is that the people inside, like you and your mommy and daddy, are healthy. In fact, the Great Separation, as it came to be known, is credited with the complete elimination of seventy-three other infectious diseases, too. Given the effects of influenza D, I daresay it was a trade-off that people were willing to make."

"And people could just meet through screens! Like us, Ms. VAIN!"

Ms. VAIN smiled. "Well, I'm not a person, but yes. And for everything you need in your apartment, there are—"

"Drones!" Cleo finished. "Daddy and I are going to paint the delivery tube like a garden."

"That will be lovely, dear. Would you like to see some pictures of a garden?"

Of course, six years later, Cleo didn't have time for pictures of gardens. And she most definitely didn't have time for a strange package, as Ms. VAIN continued to remind her every time she glanced at it instead of the double bypass surgery she was supposed to be watching.

"Cleo, you know I can tell when your eyes are not focused on me," Ms. VAIN said.

"I've watched this video a hundred times."

"Nine, actually."

"Maybe it's just the outside that's wrong?"

"Of the man's heart? I don't think so. Note the atrial—"

"Not the heart. The package."

"Really, Cleo. I must insist! I know how important the test is to you . . ."

"It *is*, Ms. VAIN. You're right. And that's exactly why I've got to figure out this box thing, so that I can study without any distractions. Right now, it's tearing my brain in two."

Ms. VAIN sighed. "The curse of the insatiably curious, I suppose."

Cleo grabbed the box and positioned it between herself and her scroll. Together, she and her teacher looked it over.

"It's a nearly perfect cube," Ms. VAIN observed.

"It looks perfect to me."

Ms. VAIN minimized herself to a corner of the screen, tossing a transparent drawing of a cube up instead. "There really isn't any such thing. At least, beyond the theoretical. Even rulers aren't exactly a foot long. If you examine one down to the molecular level—"

Cleo swiped at the air in front of Ms. VAIN to dismiss the drawing. "Now you're just trying to educate me again."

"That's my job, love," Ms. VAIN replied. "Even if I have to be sneaky about it."

She spun once in her chair, and the elderly woman suddenly appeared to be wearing a ninja's costume. Cleo giggled.

"My friend Tessa would love that. She's always wanting to play *Path of the Shadow* in the simulator."

"Too bad I can't use my ninja powers to see inside that box."

"We could open it," Cleo said, and she ran her fingers along the smooth red paper.

"It doesn't belong to you, though."

Cleo nodded. "I thought of that. But honestly, what's more likely? That a package actually got delivered to the wrong place . . ."

"That doesn't happen."

"Right, exactly! Or that the name and wrapping are just wrong? It's probably another patch of grass for my dad's office."

Ms. VAIN shrugged, which was her way of saying there were no answers to be found in the database. "I could tell you a story about a package delivered to the wrong place, if that'd help? I have access to over four thousand of them."

"No, thank you. I'm just going to . . ."

Before her courage could give out, Cleo slid a finger under the wrapping and lifted up, making a neat tear right along the seam.

"Surgical, love," Ms. VAIN said. She had dropped the

ninja costume in favor of her usual lavender blouse and sweater.

"Thanks," Cleo replied without looking up. She folded the paper down along the sides of the box carefully, figuring she could just tape it back together if she needed to. When enough of the package was revealed, Cleo set it down slowly.

"Oh no . . ."

"What is it, dear?"

Cleo picked up her scroll and held it above the package. A tiny light flickered from the corner of the screen, illuminating the clear plastic of the container. Inside, suspended carefully in stabilizing foam, were three liquid-filled spheres, their contents as blue as her father's eyes. Cleo recognized them instantly: they *were* medicine, the kind someone would put right into their injector so that it would spread as quickly as possible through their body. Tilting Ms. VAIN to the side, Cleo leaned in to read the tiny print on each sphere. When she pulled back, she repeated softly, "Oh no, no, no."

Ms. VAIN blinked. "Calotexina florinase: an anti-inflammatory compound used to treat acute and . . ."

"Fatal swelling of the brain," Cleo concluded. "Somebody does need this."

Ms. VAIN added, "And look at the expiration."

Cleo scanned the leftmost sphere. A little date had been laser-etched there: *28 May 2096.*

"It goes bad in three days," Ms. VAIN murmured.

Cleo nodded. "Somebody needs this *now.*"

CHAPTER THREE

"**E**xplain to me again why we're electing to interrupt your mother during surgery, rather than your father?"

Cleo's hands were trembling so badly that Ms. VAIN's face shimmered. She hissed, "I thought you had perfect memory . . ."

"Oh, I do, love. I could play back your answer in your own voice if you requested it. I'm just asking so that you'll be forced to think through your reasoning. You say it's because you have an emergency, and I concur, but could it also be that you've been waiting for an emergency like this just to see what it's like when your mother is working?"

Cleo stared hard at her virtual teacher.

Ms. VAIN smiled politely back.

Cleo spread her fingers like a spiderweb, then closed them on the screen. The scroll immediately rolled up tight. She set it on the couch and turned back to the door, still outlined softly in orange. With the medicine box tucked under her left arm, she reached out and took the handle.

Then she pulled, but only an inch, and pressed her face to the crack.

It was dark inside her mom's office, which only made the things that glowed seem that much more important. A rectangular table sat in the middle of the space. Cleo's mother stood over it. From the top of the table shone a pretty blue light, and that turned everything else blue, too, except for the amber lenses of her mother's goggles. Knowles Porter's hands were poised above the table, and every so often one of her fingers would flick, or her thumbs would cross. More rarely, she would say in a quiet, firm voice, "Laser four," or "suction," or "rotate camera six degrees, forward axis."

Cleo felt the hairs on her arms prickle, and she pushed the door closed as gently as she could.

"That was only two minutes, nineteen seconds," Ms. VAIN noted when Cleo unfurled her scroll.

"She was in the middle of surgery. I didn't want to startle her and risk her drone hurting the patient." *Thoughtful caring.*

"That's wise."

"But it was really amazing!" Cleo exclaimed, sliding to the floor with her back against the couch. She held her hands up, twitching the tips of her fingers just like her mom had. "You could tell how her hands controlled the drone, all those tools . . . maybe she was repairing someone's knee—it looked like she was focused on the lower left quadrant of the table." *Observant*

Ms. VAIN brought up a corner window with a three-dimensional model of a surgical drone. It looked very much like a bug, with dangly legs ending in blades, needles, and lasers. With it, Dr. Porter could help anyone, anywhere. People ordered their drones, had them delivered, and as soon as they were activated, Cleo's mom went to work. She could even chat with patients before a procedure, straight through the drone. Of course, the Surgical Council wouldn't let just anybody fly one. A person couldn't even log in to the control network without a level twenty medical clearance.

And Cleo?

She was a level zero. It would be at least another ten years before she could show her mom that she could handle a patient of her own. Someone to help. To fix. To heal.

Ten years.

Except . . .

"I wonder if Miriam Wendemore-Adisa has ever met a drone my mom piloted," she sighed, staring down at the blue spheres in the package.

"I wonder if anyone will ever get to meet a drone *you* pilot, love. If you don't pass this test, you don't get your first clearance. If you don't get your first clearance . . ."

Cleo's shoulders slumped. "I don't get level two, or three, or any of it. And all my future patients die because I failed the test. I understand."

Ms. VAIN clicked her tongue. "Now, Cleo, I think that's being a little overly dramatic."

Cleo eyed her.

"Only a little, though," her teacher conceded.

"Back to studying?" Cleo murmured.

Ms. VAIN nodded, and she brought up a series of sample questions that might be on the oral portion of the test. They worked through the list dutifully, and Cleo even began to dance as she replied, practicing her freestyle while Ms. VAIN, perched on the table, assessed her responses.

"To close a wound," Cleo panted as her feet jabbed left and right. "Hydrophobic air-activated glue, laser cauterization, and polydermal graft."

"What about rapid-absorption stitching?"

"It's ob-so-lete!" sang Cleo.

"Even in cases where the patient has an allergy to an adhesive?"

Cleo sat, gasping. "Ms. VAIN, can we talk about something else?"

"Of course."

"I want to know more about calotexina florinase."

"Cleo . . ."

"What? It's medicine! It still counts as studying!"

Ms. VAIN smiled. "It counts as studying if you're interested in it, love. One moment."

Cleo curled her toes, listening to them pop while Ms. VAIN accessed the database.

"Developed in 2061 to treat multiple types of serious and fatal brain afflictions, calotexina florinase is what is known in the medical field as a keystone drug; that is, while it can be used in conjunction with other medications as part of a treatment plan, those plans would inevitably fail without the calotexina."

Cleo shivered. "So it's essential."

"If a patient is taking it, it's because he or she can't live without it."

The weight of that thought settled so heavily on Cleo that she felt the need to physically shake it off. She leaped up, hopping and spinning until the nervous energy in her arms and legs started to dissipate. Ms. VAIN looked on calmly.

"Perhaps while you dance, we could continue with the . . . Cleo? Love?"

Cleo had frozen, one leg extended over her head, bare ankle caught in her hands. Ms. VAIN cleared her throat politely.

"Are you all right, dear?"

Cleo let her leg slowly drift back to the floor. Then she grabbed the box of medicine.

Her mom's orange light had just turned green.

"Mom! Mom!" Cleo shouted as she yanked the door open.

Dr. Porter responded to her daughter's intrusion by nearly dropping the mug of tea in her hands. A fair amount sloshed onto the floor before she managed to find her grip. Cleo skidded to a stop near the surgical table.

"You're . . . you're done, right, Mom?" Cleo asked breathlessly.

Dr. Porter put the mug down slowly, shaking her hands

and then wiping them on her pants. Once they were dry, she reached up to ease her goggles off her eyes.

"It's a good thing I let that tea get cold," she sighed. "And no. I'm taking a five-minute break, three of which are likely to be me checking to make sure there are no droplets of hibiscus on my table."

"Sorry, Mom," Cleo said. "I'll help!"

Dr. Porter jumped in front of her daughter.

"No! Don't move your hands over the surface. My drone is on pause. Any movement over the table might activate her."

Cleo stepped back. "I could get some towels?"

Her mom shook her head, a mountain of brown-and-gray curls threatening to burst forth from the net that held it at bay. "It'll be okay, Cleo. What's so important that you're interrupting me—"

"This!" Cleo exclaimed, shoving the clear container into her mother's hands. "It's for Miriam Wendemore-Adisa. Who is she?"

Dr. Porter's lips pursed as she rotated the box. "This is medicine for . . ."

"Brain swelling! And it expires in three days!"

"How did we get it?"

"It got delivered through our tube. The package had our address, but the name was Miriam Wendemore-Adisa. Is she one of your patients?"

Dr. Porter handed the box back to Cleo, who took it with both hands. Her mom picked her tea mug up and took a thoughtful sip. The blue-and-yellow eye logo of the Surgical Council, stenciled on the mug, stared down at Cleo, just above the solid letters of their motto: COMPASSION. PRECISION. PERFECTION. It made Cleo a bit uneasy, so she looked away.

"I don't have a patient by that name," Dr. Porter said.

Cleo nodded. "Yeah. See? It got delivered to us by mistake!"

"The delivery drones don't make mistakes, baby," her mom said hurriedly. A blue light had begun to emanate from the top of the surgical table.

"What are we going to do?" Cleo asked, shifting from foot to foot.

"Nothing right now. I have to get back to surgery."

"But won't this lady die without—"

Dr. Porter held up a finger. "Very important lesson, Cleo. You deal with the patient on your table first."

"But, Mom!"

Dr. Porter leaned forward, pressing her lips to Cleo's forehead. "You have my permission to get on the network to figure this out. Do some research. Let your father and me know how it went at dinner. For now, though, bye."

CHAPTER FOUR

Cleo trudged back to the living room. The door closed automatically behind her, and the orange seal reappeared. Flumping down on the couch, she held the box of medicine up to the ceiling light, watching the blue beams that filtered through the medicine play across the white cushions. It was sort of mesmerizing, and she felt her heart relax, if only a bit. Then she flipped herself until her hair tumbled off the edge and her bottom pressed into the back of the couch. Her feet in the air, she angled her left big toe toward the wall behind the sofa and touched the surface. A black window appeared, and a cheerful boy's voice said, "Lattimore Network Solutions. Where would you like to go today?" The menu kid sounded eager and a tad mischievous, just like always.

"Call Miriam Wendemore-Adisa."

"Password required for peer-to-peer connection."

Cleo wrinkled her nose. She didn't have her parents' password. Instead, she tried, "Drone Transport, please."

Before she had even finished her sentence, the screen was filled with a menu of options. Most of them were categories of items to order: food, clothes, replacement parts for things in the apartment. Some were for services: repairs, cleaning drones, and such. Cleo scanned the menu, which progressed downward as she twitched her foot in the air. After a few moments, she spotted what she was looking for and said, "Speak with a Drone Transport representative."

The window went blank momentarily, and then a young man's head appeared. He was dressed in an outfit that resembled an old-time postal worker's, complete with a boxy hat and a blue button-down shirt.

"Drone Transport," he said. "How can I help you?"

Cleo stared up at him from her awkward, upside-down perch on the couch. He, in turn, stared forward and smiled. His teeth were absolutely perfect.

"Are you real?" Cleo asked.

"No!" he replied, as excited about that fact as a kid announcing it was her birthday. "But my conversation tree has over seventy-two million branches, and I'm programmed to assist with thousands of issues."

Cleo waved her foot in his face. He didn't react. After a few silent moments, he said, "Are you still there? How can I help you?"

Rolling up into a kneel, Cleo said, "We got a package by mistake."

"Ah! I understand that you need help with something you ordered by mistake. Please state your—"

"No. We didn't order it. It just came, even though it doesn't belong to us."

"To return an item you ordered by mistake, please notify our service drone department. They will be happy to send a carrier to pick up your item. Simply place it in your tube . . ."

Cleo pressed her palm to her forehead.

"Wait. What I'm saying is we got a delivery meant for someone else. You gave us another person's medicine."

There was a pause, and the grinning man blinked several times. Then he said, "Drone Transport! How can I help you?"

"With this!" Cleo snarled, and she held the medicine up to the screen.

"I see you have a package. What would you like to do with it? I can repeat an order, track it, find objects like it—"

"Track it," Cleo demanded.

"Okay! I'll track your package. Please say the six-digit address to which the package is addressed, or you can hold the address label up to your screen's visual array."

Gritting her teeth, Cleo said, "I don't need to know where it went. I need to know where it was supposed to go."

"I see you have a package! What would—"

"Gah!" Cleo hopped off the couch and stalked over to where she left the glossy red paper. She picked it up and smoothed it out, then slapped it against the visual array.

"Great!" the man chirped. "I see your package has been delivered. It arrived at ten thirty-seven a.m. on May twenty-fifth."

"Yes, it was delivered, but it's not mine. I'm Cleo Porter. My mom is Dr. Knowles Porter. My dad is Bowman Porter. This package is for Miriam Wendemore-Adisa. She doesn't live here."

"Cleo Porter! Hello! Your address is 412263. Your package was delivered to 412263 at ten thirty-seven a.m. on May twenty-fifth. We are glad it arrived satisfactorily! Is there anything else we can help you with?"

"Close network," Cleo growled, and the wall shifted back to its usual creamy white. She felt a burble of anger wriggling around in her stomach, so she carefully set down the medicine and snapped off a few high-leg kicks, just to get the energy out. Her last pivot brought her near her father's work door, which was lined with the same orange light as her mother's office. There was no hesitation this time, though; as far as Cleo was concerned, simulator programming was an eminently interruptible profession. She yanked the door open, said, "Daddy! I need you!" and barged right in.

CHAPTER FIVE

"Theo! Perfect!" her father said. "I need a test subject."

Mr. Porter, a round, bald, and perpetually happy man, had a habit of biting his tongue gently when he was deep in thought, so this wasn't the first time Cleo had heard him misfire on her name. She ignored it.

"Can it wait? I have something really important to talk to you about."

Between the two of them was a long counter, similar to the one in their kitchen. Every inch of it was covered in planters, and from each sprouted thick patches of grass. Some of the blades were tall and straight, like the bristles on Cleo's toothbrush. Others were soft, droopy, and tangled, sort of like her hair on a tricky morning. The patch her father was stroking with a gloved hand was brown and brittle. Cleo could hear it scratching the padding of the glove.

"Cleopatra Porter, you know I'm on deadline."

She stuck out her chin and stared at her father, her arms crossed.

"Fine," he said. "I'll make a deal with you. I'll let you go first, if you promise to hop in the simulator afterward and give me your absolutely honest opinion."

Cleo nodded. "Deal."

Mr. Porter stepped away from the counter, carefully working his gloves off each finger before setting the pair on a little stand at his desk. Then he collapsed into his chair, kicked his feet up, and laced his fingers behind his head. "What's got my girl so fired up? Test stress?"

Cleo shook her head. "No. Or yes, but that's not why I need you."

"Good!" he said, laughing. "Because you've got more knowledge about the human body in your pinkie than I do in . . . well . . . here!"

Cleo arched an eyebrow as her father patted his stomach. "Dad, that's not where . . ."

"Here?" Mr. Porter continued, pointing at his elbow.

"Dad!"

"Ohh, right! Up here!" he exclaimed, and finally pointed to his temple. "See? Told you I don't know much about—"

"I get it, Dad. Funny." has humor

"Not funny enough, I guess," he said, pouting at his daughter's stern expression. "Guess you really do have something serious on your mind."

Cleo circled the counter, running her fingertips over

the different kinds of grass. "Yeah. We got a package of medicine that doesn't belong to us. It had our address on there, but it's meant for someone named Miriam."

"Maybe your mother ordered it?"

"I asked. She said—"

Mr. Porter sat up so quickly he nearly fell out of his chair. "You didn't interrupt her during surgery, did you?"

Cleo waved him off. "No! I'd never!" she insisted, a tickly blush spreading up her neck and into her cheeks. She wasn't about to mention the peek-in. "Her light was green, so I talked to her during her five-minute break. Mom didn't order the medicine. They just messed up the delivery."

Mr. Porter eased back, stroking his mustache with two fingers. It was as thick as some of the best grass samples on the counter. "That's not possible, honey." Everything

Cleo rolled her eyes. "Everyone keeps saying that. Why digital is it impossible?" nothing messes up

"Has no one explained to you how transport drones work?"

"I've never asked. Ms. VAIN probably has a story or two hundred . . ."

Opening a drawer, Mr. Porter rummaged until he found a stylus. He double-tapped the surface of his desk, and it lit up. Cleo shuffled over and cleared a few papers away so she could sit on the corner.

"Here's our apartment, right?" he said, and he drew a square on the surface of the desk. It was messy—more like a blob—but the desk recognized it and fixed it for him. "And here's our tube. The transports aren't like surgical drones. Nobody flies them. They're automated."

"I know that," Cleo said impatiently.

"Of course you do. You're a genius!" Mr. Porter replied proudly. "But what you might not know is how they operate. Each apartment has its own signal—a unique signature."

"Our address?"

"Yes, but it's not like the old days, where it just meant your position relative to your neighbors. It's an actual code, and that code only gets transmitted to a drone if someone inside the apartment orders something. You can't send a box, or a gift, or grass, or anything to someone else."

Cleo nodded. "They were worried about contamination, I bet."

"That'd be my guess, too. Influenza D scared a lot of people, and from what I've read and your mother has told me, they were right to be afraid."

"So we only get things that we order?" Cleo asked.

"Correct. And our tube will only open for a drone that has our specific code. You couldn't even mess it up if you tried, since the code is given by the apartment itself. Say to the grocery program, 'I'd like a dozen carrots, and I live at 111111,' and we'd still get the carrots here ten minutes later."

"It's like our home sends the order, not us."

Cleo's dad reached out and tapped her forehead. "Exactly."

Swiping the stylus from his hand, Cleo drew a big

circle around their apartment. "Well, then how did we get Miriam Wendemore-Adisa's medicine?"

"That, kid, is a real mystery. Maybe you should research it! You can hop on the network once we're—"

"Mom said the same thing."

"Smart lady."

Cleo sighed loudly.

Mr. Porter patted her knee. "It'll be okay. If this Miriam lady's medicine doesn't show up, she'll just reorder it, I'm sure."

"I don't know, Dad . . . it's not like aspirin or something. It's calotexina florinase, a keystone medicine. That means—"

"I get it. It's important, which is why I have total confidence that you'll figure out what to do. I wish I could help more, but I've got my own problems here. For instance, this contract, which I'm already a week late in fulfilling."

Cleo nodded, but she still felt off. Reaching up, she ran her fingers along her shoulder. It felt as hard as the desk beneath her. Even when she thought about the level-one Surgical Council test, when she really let the weight of its impending arrival settle on her, her trapezius muscles didn't tighten as badly as this. She closed her eyes and tried to will her head into a more comfortable position, to adjust her spine like her dance instruction videos showed her, but instead of imagining the muscles of her upper back working in harmony to calm her, she saw a terrible thing: an old woman, stricken and shaking on the ground. Above her, the broad grin of the Drone Transport man loomed, his voice barking, "How can I help you? How can I help you? How can . . ."

"Your turn, Cleo. Hop into the simulator for me."

Cleo shook her head to clear the image away and looked up. The outside of the huge, boxy simulator was covered in wires, cooling tubes, and control panels. Inside, it seemed like her father had simply conjured up the middle of a field. The sky was sunny, a few trees swayed in the distance, and she could hear the wind as it tickled along the grass.

"See the brown patch on the counter?" Mr. Porter asked.

Cleo did—it was the same patch he'd been playing with when she came in. She had helped her father enough to know what to do, so she stuck her hand into the middle of the blades, feeling their dry, crinkly texture. When she bent one in two, she expected it to break like an uncooked noodle, but it gently folded instead, a little crack appearing right at the joint. Flattening her hand, she pressed down, letting the individual pieces poke into her palm. She kept it there for a few moments, then said, "Got it, Dad."

"Good. You can head on in."

The entrance to the simulator was an arch. It was normally sealed with a zip-up plastic curtain, but her dad had pinned it open for her, and she was able to walk right in. As soon as she did, everything changed. Where before she'd been a little chilly, now she was pleasantly warm, the artificial sunlight shining across her cheeks and arms. A piped-in breeze swirled and tangled her curls around her face, so she slipped a hand into her pocket for a band and pulled her hair back into a loose ponytail.

"How does the grass feel?" her dad called from just outside. She couldn't see him, of course: as soon as he had closed and zipped the curtain, the simulator had read it as a writable surface, and it had extended the three-dimensional image of the field to cover that as well. As far as Cleo's eyes knew, she was standing in an open field on a beautiful afternoon. She took a deep breath and exhaled. It even smelled like grass.

"Cool. Fresh. Soft," Cleo replied as she wiggled her toes. "It's really good, Dad. About the med—"

"One second, honey. What you're feeling now is the usual program. But I'm going for dry grass today. It's for a new soccer simulation; they want the players to be able to experience a variety of fields. I'm going to shift the scene to one in late October. Hold on."

Cleo closed her eyes—scene transitions always made her dizzy. She felt the wind change first. It shifted directions, and it got cold enough to raise goose bumps along her arms. She imagined it would feel good to a bunch of sweaty soccer players in their simulators. The glow of the sun changed, too, and she could tell through her eyelids that it had gotten just a shade darker. The biggest change, though, was beneath her feet. Instead of the cool freshness of before, she felt a prickle, just different enough to be uncomfortable.

"You can open your eyes, Cleo," her father said, and so she did.

The trees were still there, but they blazed red and yellow. And the sun was lower in the sky. She wrapped her arms around herself instinctively and looked down. The grass was much lower and scragglier, and all of it was brown.

"How does it feel now?"

Cleo eased a foot forward. Beneath her, the weight-sensitive plates of the simulator read her movement and produced static electricity to fill in the gaps between her skin and the floor. The idea—one that her father had perfected for fresh, evenly trimmed grass—was that the static should be just strong enough, and manipulated into just the right patterns, that it should feel identical to the dry grass Cleo had touched on the counter.

"Still a little cottony," Cleo said. To be sure, she knelt down and passed her hand over the grass. The visual receptors picked up her movement just fine; the grass seemed to bend beneath her fingertips as she was touching it. And it felt like she was touching *something*, but it wasn't quite brittle enough; the individual blades weren't defined as sharply as they could be.

"Cottony, eh?" Mr. Porter mumbled as he unzipped the curtain. His shiny head suddenly popped in, as if appearing from the sky itself. Cleo yipped.

"Didn't mean to scare you!"

"It's okay. And yeah, it feels a bit soft and spread out. Now can we—"

Her dad cut her off with a raised finger. As she shifted

impatiently, Mr. Porter knelt and passed a hand over the sensor plates. Then he frowned.

"Yep. Cottony. I'll have to refocus the pattern optimizer and pull back on the volume for now. I'll need a new sample, too. The one I have is wilting fast."

"What if you could just go outside and get some?"

Mr. Porter snorted. "No, thank you very much! A box of scratchy grass isn't worth a case of influenza D."

"But nobody's had influenza D for years!"

"In here, Cleo," Mr. Porter said, and he reached up to tousle her hair. She swatted his hand away.

"Whoa!"

Cleo winced. "Sorry, Dad. I didn't mean to . . ."

Mr. Porter shook his head. "No. I get it. This medicine thing has you pretty worked up."

Cleo nodded.

"Tell you what. I suppose I can afford a little break. I'll go out and see about calling this Miriam Wendemore-Adisa lady for you."

Cleo took a deep breath. "Thanks."

"Anything else I can do?"

"Since you're not going to be using the sim, could I maybe see if any of my friends are on?"

"What about the test?"

"I studied for four hours this morning, and Ms. VAIN is going to double-quiz me tonight before bed."

"You think that's enough?"

Cleo sighed. "Probably not, but with this weird package thing, my mind is all over the place. I just want to say hi to Tessa or something."

Mr. Porter nodded. "Fair enough. Ten minutes, Cleo, but then I need it back."

"Okay!"

"I'm going to go get a snack, too. You need anything?"

"I'm good. I had an apple."

As he rezipped the curtain, Cleo's dad said, "The core of which I most certainly won't find in the middle of the floor, right?"

Cleo blushed. "Only if you don't look very hard . . ."

Mr. Porter muttered something else, and then Cleo heard his door shut. She was alone.

But not for long.

CHAPTER SIX

"**E**nd simulation," Cleo commanded, and the field disappeared. The wind stopped. Her feet felt only smooth plastic beneath her, and the cool of autumn was replaced by the stillness of her own apartment. She allowed herself a little shiver.

"Find Tessa Prince."

A black window, similar to the one that had appeared above their couch, snapped open on the wall in front of her. According to the drop-down list of her friends, Tessa was playing *Kitten Trainer*. Cleo grumbled jealously; she wished she had time for a simulator pet.

"Page Tessa."

After a few moments, a message appeared:

TESSA HAS REQUESTED A MEETING ON THE GREEN

Cleo closed her eyes tightly, and then said, "Accept request."

The simulator whirred to life, and Cleo immediately felt the sun on her skin once more. Fresh green grass—programmed by her father, Cleo thought proudly—seemed to sprout beneath her feet, and the sounds of birds chirping and other kids talking gradually built around her. A sudden pressure on her upper arm clued her in that the transition was complete—Tessa had poked her.

"Cleo Porter . . . On sim five days before her test . . . I didn't think I'd get to see you for another month!" Tessa exclaimed. The girl, taller than Cleo and sporting the most impressively defined calf muscles of anyone she'd ever seen, sat in the grass and patted the ground. Cleo reached out to pass a hand over Tessa's spiky blond hair. It felt more like the brown grass than her dad's simulation had.

"This is new," Cleo said as she joined her friend.

"Things change when you don't come to the Green for weeks."

Cleo nodded. "Have you seen any other kids in the surgical track lately?"

Tessa shook her head and waved at a fly that buzzed around her. "Suspend insects!" she snapped, and the fly disappeared, as did the low chittering of cicadas that Cleo had barely even noticed was there. "And no. You're the first I've seen in a while. Taking a break?"

Cleo shrugged. "Sort of. Dad's letting me use the sim for ten minutes while he gets a snack."

"Then you better tell me everything quick!" Tessa whispered, leaning in. "What's the latest gruesome surgery your mom had to do? And did you get to watch the playback?"

"Not now, Tess. I need to ask you about something."

Tessa pouted.

"This is serious, and stranger than surgeries."

"Weirder than that lady's tumor with the teeth inside?"

"It's called a teratoma, and yes. We got a package delivered to our apartment, and it's not ours."

"Shut your virtual mouth!" Tessa gasped.

"Honest!"

"That's not supposed to happen!"

Cleo crossed her arms.

"Which, I'm guessing, a few people have already told you," Tessa said, holding up her hands.

"My dad gave me a full lecture on how drone deliveries work. There were pictures and everything."

"Did you try the Drone Transport help menu?"

Cleo winced. "Yeah. Tried that, too."

"Well." Tessa shrugged, shoving a finger through the static-grass beneath her to feel the smoothness of her simulator's floor. "I guess there's not much else to do. Maybe enjoy your free stuff?"

"Can't. It's medicine."

"Whoa," Tessa murmured, and she sat up.

"*Critical* medicine. For all I know, this lady, Miriam Wendemore-Adisa, is dying while I'm sitting in my living room fooling around with her meds and studying for my test."

"I'm glad I'm in general studies. No big test until I'm seventeen, and I don't get life-or-death boxes sent to my tube . . ."

Cleo threw herself backward in frustration, lying there and looking up at the faux sky. "That's one of the worst parts—I can't concentrate on the one without obsessing over the other."

"What did your mom say? She's the surgeon."

Slipping her hands behind her head, Cleo muttered, "'You deal with the patient on your table first.'"

"Well, there's your answer, right?" Tessa said.

"Huh?"

"You've got her meds. You're worried about her. I'd say Miriam . . ."

"Wendemore-Adisa."

"Yeah! I'd say she's your patient!"

Cleo snorted. Tessa stared at her, lips pressed together and eyebrows raised. Cleo tried to ignore her, but Tessa was unflinching. Gradually, Cleo sat up, rubbing her hand along her shoulder again.

"Okay," she said finally. "What do I do?"

Tessa exhaled and shrugged. "I dunno. But you've got to do *something*. You'll drive yourself mad if you don't. I *know* you—remember when we played *DragonSim 3* a few years ago? We never made it out of the first village, because you insisted on treating the wounds of every townsperson the dragon had injured."

"I was the healer, and they needed medical attention!"

"They weren't real, and there were two hundred of them!"

Cleo pouted. "Two hundred nineteen. And I saved most of them."

Tessa threw her hands up. "The point is, you aren't going to leave this alone. You've got to fix it."

Cleo nodded. "I do, don't I? But where do I even start?"

"I . . . I don't know. I mean, it's not like you can just shout for someone named Miriam and hope they show up."

Cleo smiled, but a sudden thought wiped it out. She looked around the Green. Just like Tessa and her, the other pockets of students strolling, lounging, or reading were kids who had access to the VAIN database. And just like she had found Tessa, Cleo could check the online status of anyone who used it.

"Tess, what if Miriam Wendemore-Adisa is a student?"

Tessa gasped. "Oh! You're right! Let me!"

Coming up to her knees, Cleo's friend reached out, pointing toward the horizon. To Cleo, it looked like Tessa's index finger had met with an invisible wall, the tip bending upward and turning pink. She knew that meant Tessa was touching the actual wall of her own simulator, but it was still strange to see. As she watched, Tessa drew a rectangle with that finger, which caused the black menu screen to appear in both of their versions of the Green. Cleo scooted up next to Tessa, ignoring the shiver of static that grazed along her arm as they touched.

"Find Miriam Wendemore-Adisa," Tessa said excitedly.

Both girls watched, eyes wide.

NO USER IN SYSTEM BY THAT NAME *not a student*

Cleo took a steadying breath. "Last online: Miriam Wendemore-Adisa."

NO USER BY THAT NAME HAS LOGGED ON

Both girls sat back on their ankles.

"That was . . . ," Tessa began.

"Worth a shot," Cleo finished. "But now what?"

Tessa nibbled at the corner of her pinkie as she thought. Then her whole face lit up.

"What?" Cleo asked.

"Tell me about the conversation you had with Drone Transport."

"Ugh. Do I have to?"

Tessa nodded. Cleo grumbled her way through the story.

"Yeah. That sounds about right," Tessa said. "And it gives me an idea."

"Am I going to like it?"

Tessa grinned mischievously.

"That depends on how comfortable you are with lying . . ."

CHAPTER SEVEN

Cleo kissed her father on the cheek on her way out of his office. He smelled like peaches.

"No luck on contacting that lady. Sorry, Cleo."

"That's okay, Dad. Thanks for trying!"

"Guess that means it's back to studying?"

"Yep!" Cleo said, far too cheerfully.

Her father narrowed his eyes at her, but then laughed, shrugged, and closed the door to his office, pausing to say through the crack, "Just don't get into too much trouble."

Cleo exhaled sharply, glad Tessa hadn't seen that little exchange. It would have told her friend everything she needed to know about how well Cleo could lie. Even with the stakes as high as they were, she didn't feel comfortable trying to fool another person.

Fortunately for her, the man she was about to talk to wasn't a person at all.

"Drone Transport!" the chipper postal guy said. "How can I help you?"

"Hi," Cleo responded, swallowing. "My name is . . . um . . . Miriam Wendemore-Adisa."

"Good afternoon, Miss Miriam Wendemore-Adisa!"

Cleo wrung her hands. "Yes. Good afternoon. I have a question about a package."

"Thank you, Miss Miriam Wendemore-Adisa. I understand that you have a question about a package. What information would you like? You can say, 'Schedule a delivery,' 'Track a package,' 'Delivery history,' or something else."

"Track a package, please."

"Okay! I can see you're calling from 412263. Which delivery would you—"

"Um, no," Cleo blurted. "That's . . . that's not right. I'm Miriam Wendemore-Adisa. Some . . . other people live at 412263. But not me. Can you tell me *my* address?"

The man blinked, then blinked again. He never stopped smiling, though.

"I can see you're calling from 412263," he eventually repeated.

Cleo groaned. Then she said, "Schedule a delivery."

"Absolutely! What would you like to order? I can show you a menu, or you can say, 'Repeat a delivery.'"

"Repeat a delivery!" Cleo gasped excitedly.

"Okay! Please choose one of the following items to deliver again."

A menu appeared next to the man's face. At the top

of the list was the calotexina florinase, followed by several grocery orders.

"Item one, please!"

The man blinked several times, then said, "I'm sorry. You have reached your maximum number of orders for that product this month. Would you like to order something else?"

"Crap!" Cleo said under her breath.

"I'm sorry. We do not offer that product at this time. Would you like to order something else?"

Cleo blushed, imagining Tessa laughing herself sick. That vision was quickly replaced by the one of Miriam Wendemore-Adisa suffering, and Cleo shivered. Tears welled at the corners of her eyes, and she reached up to dab at them with her wrist. The Drone Transport guy grinned at her.

"Delivery history," Cleo whispered.

"Great! I can help you with that. Getting delivery history."

A few blinks later, and the man's face disappeared entirely, replaced by a drop-down list of everything Miriam Wendemore-Adisa had ordered in the last month. Like the repeat-a-delivery menu, it was mostly groceries. As far as Cleo could tell, there was nothing there to help her— certainly no other medications she could try to reorder and have sent to Miriam's address . . . if such a thing was even possible. Based on what her dad had told her, whatever she ordered was bound to just show up in their own tube twenty minutes later.

"This is hopeless!" Cleo spat, and she spun around to collapse on the couch.

"I'm sorry, that's not an item on your delivery history."

"Shut up!" she shouted, throwing an arm over her eyes.

"I'm sorry, that's not an item on your delivery history. You can say, 'Almonds,' or 'Celery,' or 'Knitting needles' . . ."

"I don't need any stupid knitting needles!"

"Okay! Knitting needles! Your order of knitting needles was delivered to 631445 at three twenty-four p.m. on May eleventh. We are glad it arrived satisfactorily! Is there anything else we can help you with?"

Cleo sat up so quickly her ponytail whipped over and smacked her across the eyes.

"Please repeat that?"

"Okay! Your order . . ."

As he happily obeyed, Cleo scrambled to find her scroll. She snapped it open, whispered her voice ID phrase, and pointed it at the Drone Transport guy.

"Ms. VAIN: Record!"

Dutifully, Ms. VAIN obliged.

CHAPTER EIGHT

S croll in one hand and the box of medicine in the other, Cleo rushed down the hall to her bedroom, panting as she closed the door and slid to the ground. She felt her own pulse: nearly a hundred beats per minute, or almost what she hit after a full session of dance in the simulator. And it showed no sign of slowing.

Normally, Cleo's bedroom was her refuge. She had even taken to studying in the living room so that she wouldn't come to associate the stress of the test with this place. Sure, it was hard to avoid thinking about it no matter where she was, and the six-foot-tall skeleton dominating the back corner didn't help matters, but it was easier to sleep at night with a bit of emotional separation. Now, though, none of it seemed to help: not the gentle blue of her bedsheets, not the shrubs and flowers her father had painted around the baseboards, not even the silky blanket draped over the back of her chair.

She had Miriam Wendemore-Adisa's address.

And no clue what to do with it.

"Stupid influenza D," she growled.

Ms. VAIN, who was forced to stare up at the ceiling, asked, "What's that, love?"

"If there had never been influenza D, I could get a drone to take this package to Miriam, no problem."

"If there had never been influenza D, there's really no telling what the world might look like. Given the elevation in your heart rate, I'm not so sure dwelling on it is the healthiest thing for you, dear."

"I can't help it, Ms. VAIN! It's all I can think about. Well, not influenza D, but this package. It's basically drilled a hole in my head and laid eggs in my mind!"

"That's a lurid parasite reference. Nicely done!"

"Thanks," Cleo said dryly. "It still doesn't help me get this medicine where it needs to go."

"Would it help if I pointed out some of the other positives about the Great Separation? Because people no longer travel, fossil fuel use has declined dramatically, and it is estimated that over three million square miles of deforested land has been reclaimed by vegetation. The climate has stabilized, too, with—"

benefits

"All that is great, Ms. VAIN, but there might as well be three million miles between me and Miriam Wendemore-Adisa."

"Yes, pity you can't just take it to her yourself, like in the stories."

Cleo left Ms. VAIN on the floor as she got up and launched herself into bed. She landed facedown on her pillow, grabbing Elly the Elephant along the way. She let the darkness and the clean smell of her sheets fight the buzzing in her brain, and it helped—at least a little. After a few moments, she lifted her head, squinting down at the light shining from her scroll, which still lay flat on her floor.

"What stories?" Cleo asked.

"There are many, love. Quests to deliver things are as old as storytelling itself. According to some, men have run many miles to warn cities of an impending attack. Brave heroes have overcome all odds to return that which was lost. Rings have been delivered to volcanoes, slippers have found their rightful feet, and the moon has been taken back to the sky."

Cleo couldn't resist. She tucked Elly against her side and slid to the floor, just as she had when she was little.

"What is the most famous?"

"That's a matter of opinion, but the one I have the most versions of—across oral retellings, books, poems, stage works, and screenplays—is 'Little Red Riding Hood.'"

"Tell it to me?"

Ms. VAIN blinked, then chuckled warmly. "I have, dearest. Three times. But you were much younger, and you tended to fall asleep before I even got to the wolf."

"There's a wolf?"

"Oh yes, though in some versions it's a man—a robber or some such scoundrel. In one it's a snapping turtle. But in ninety-two percent of the 312,556 versions I have on file, the antagonist is a wolf."

Cleo crossed her legs, laid her scroll across her lap, and settled in. "Can you give me your own version?"

Ms. VAIN nodded. "Certainly. I can compile the most common elements from all of them and distill a telling. It might lack some of the flourishes of the original iterations, though. There's a movie version in which the entire cast raps, if you'd prefer to see that."

Cleo smiled. "Maybe some other time. Your story should be fine."

"As you wish," Ms. VAIN said, and she reached down below her desk. After a moment of shuffling and searching, she produced a beautiful tome, heavy enough to thud when she settled it on her desk. The cover was a fine, rich maroon, and the pages themselves were a glimmering gold. Along the spine, in thick, bold medieval lettering, it said:

A Taille of a Journey Most Perilous: Lyttle Red Rydyng Hoode

"So dramatic, Ms. VAIN," Cleo teased.

"You would prefer a pamphlet?"

Cleo shook her head. "No. I like it."

"Good," Ms. VAIN said, and she lifted the cover slowly. "It's storytelling. It should be dramatic, darling."

Adjusting her bifocals and licking her thumb, Ms. VAIN turned the first page and began.

"Once upon a time, there was a young girl, no older than you. She and her mother lived in a little village at the edge of a great woods. Her name was Little Red Riding Hood, and—"

"Wait. That was her name?"

Ms. VAIN looked up. "Yes, in most versions—particularly those developed in the twentieth century and beyond. Some simply call her Red, or Little Red Cap. There are a few Valeries, Sarahs, and, appropriately, Rubys mixed in, but the vast majority stick with Little Red Riding Hood."

Cleo looked skeptically down at her own clothes.

"That'd be like if my parents named me Medium Gray Sitting Pants."

"Would you like me to call you that from now on?"

Cleo cringed.

"I'll take that as a no, then. Shall I continue?"

"Yes, please. And you can just call her Red."

Ms. VAIN cleared her throat. "As I was saying, *Red lived with her mother. One day, after a morning of baking, Red decided that it would be a gracious gesture to take a basket of treats to her ailing grandmother, who lived in the middle of the forest.* You'll likely be interested to know, Cleo, that in many versions, the basket included medicine."

"Whoa," Cleo murmured appreciatively, and she glanced at the blue spheres in the box by the door.

"*Red's mother,* who is unnamed—"

"Call her Stumptoe Poutybottom."

"Are you serious?"

Cleo grinned. "Might as well."

Ms. VAIN stared at her over her glasses. "Let me get this straight, child . . . you take issue with 'Little Red Riding Hood,' but you have no quarrel with 'Stumptoe'?"

"Poutybottom. And no. I think it's dignified."

Ms. VAIN pursed her lips. "Remind me later to read you the definition of 'dignified.'"

"Sure. Anyway, Mrs. Poutybottom was about to do something."

"Yes. *Stumptoe cheered her daughter for her thoughtfulness but warned her of the dangers in the woods: 'There are wolves and other creatures that would do you harm. Do not stray from the path, but speed directly to Grandmother's house.' Red assured her mother that she would be safe, and off she went.*

"At the edge of the wood, just before the darkened trailhead, a hunter leaned against a tree. Echoing Mrs. Poutybottom's advice, he warned Red that he had heard the howling of a wolf on his last venture down the path, so she ought to be particularly careful."

Ms. VAIN paused, pushing up her glasses. "I should say, Cleo, that these old fairy tales do tend to get a bit pedantic in their insistence on a moral."

"Yes, I get it. The woods are bad. Wolves are scary. Be careful."

"Just so. And Red *was* careful . . . at least, until she actually met the wolf. He was sly, and he was charming."

"He talked?"

"Yes. And he convinced Red that a bouquet of flowers would do her grandmother a world of good. *While Red foolishly fell for the distraction, the wolf seized the opportunity to race ahead to Grandmother's house. He barged in, ate the grandmother, then took her place. When Red finally arrived, it was the wolf who greeted her, dressed in Grandmother's bedclothes.*"

Cleo arched an eyebrow. "Where was Red's grandpa? Or her dad, for that matter?"

"Neither is a character in ninety-nine percent of the versions I have in the database."

"And Red didn't recognize that it wasn't her grandmother?"

"Oh, she did. Wouldn't you?"

Ms. VAIN lifted the book and turned it around. A picture at the bottom of the page enlarged, taking up the entire screen. It showed a red-hooded girl standing at the foot of a patchwork-quilted bed. The covers were drawn up, but the muzzle of a wolf poked forward, clearly visible beneath a blue bonnet.

"*Red noticed immediately, and she skeptically inquired about the wolf's eyes, ears, and, ultimately, teeth. At just that moment, the wolf swallowed her whole.*"

"Yeesh!" Cleo said. "That's a terrible ending!"

"It's not the end, love. *With a belly full of human flesh, the wolf fell into a contented slumber. His snores attracted the attention of the hunter, who crept in, slit the wolf's stomach open, and freed both Red and her grandmother.*"

"They were alive?"

"Very much so—and well enough to stuff the wolf's gut with rocks, then sew him closed. When he woke up—"

"He survived that, too?!"

"It's a fairy tale, dear, so yes . . . though not for long. *Seeing the hunter, the wolf attempted to flee, but his abdomen was so laden with rocks that he tired quickly, and he died of exhaustion outside the house. His fur was made into a new cloak for Red, and, as they all tended to do, they lived happily ever after.*"

"So many questions . . . ," Cleo mumbled.

"I can answer them, though it all boils down to reminding children to be wary of strangers and the woods."

"Red did deliver the medicine, though, right?"

Ms. VAIN nodded. "She did, yes."

"And the grandmother survived?"

"In over ninety-five percent of the versions, yes."

Cleo put her hands atop her head and looked at the ceiling.

"Happily ever after . . ."

"What's that, dear?"

Cleo closed her eyes, imagining the story. Then, like a sharp breath, an idea filled her mind. It was one that had been drifting just around the edges for hours. Now, though, it rushed in, setting her neurons to crackling and hands to trembling.

"Maybe that's not the moral," she said softly.

"The story is pretty clear in that regard, Cleo. The wolf is danger personified, the woods a consistent metaphor for the unknown."

"Yes," Cleo conceded. "But Red goes anyway. She even gets eaten, but she still delivers the medicine, and in the end, she's okay. What if the lesson isn't to avoid the wolves and woods, but to do what's right in spite of them?"

"Cleo . . ."

"Ms. VAIN," Cleo murmured as she crawled over to the box of calotexina florinase. She picked it up with both hands and held it close to her chest. "I'm going to deliver this medicine." Decision

"But, dear, how on earth are you going to do that?"

Cleo stood up, eyes roving about her room. She looked at the bed, the desk, the skeleton, and Elly the Elephant. Finally, she looked down at Ms. VAIN, who waited patiently, her head tilted softly to the side.

Slipping back to her knees, Cleo sighed. "I have no idea . . ."

CHAPTER NINE

Two hours later, Ms. VAIN's face was covered in scribbled-out plans. She had graciously volunteered her space for Cleo's work, partially so that she could observe, correct, and caution Cleo after nearly every line she drew. The latest notion took up the entire screen: Hypnotize Dr. Porter to get her surgical drone password, order a drone to be dropped off at Cleo's apartment, tie the package to its back, and then fly it through their tube to wherever it needed to go. Ms. VAIN had complimented Cleo on her creativity, but as soon as the virtual teacher had pointed out that the drone was probably too small to carry the package, that they didn't know if the drone's battery carried enough charge to complete the journey, that once it reached Miriam Wendemore-Adisa's apartment it had no way of getting in without her code, and that Cleo had no earthly clue how to hypnotize someone anyway, Cleo had crossed that plan out, too. In fact, the only one of Cleo's dozen schemes that had lingered was *Bring the medicine there myself.*

That, though, invited questions like a flower did bees.

"How do I get out?" Cleo wondered aloud. "And once I do, how do I find Miriam? And what should I bring? What if it's a long trip? What if I get lost? How do I make it home again? What's it like out there? What if I miss the test?"

Ms. VAIN kept opening her mouth to answer, but Cleo had a new question ready before she could respond to the last. Eventually, she sighed loudly enough to cut Cleo off.

"Perhaps leaving well enough alone—"

"It's not well enough!" Cleo shouted. It was louder than she meant it to be, and she clapped her hands over her mouth. She noticed they were cold and trembling against the warmth of her lips. "Sorry, Ms. VAIN. I didn't mean to yell. But Miriam Wendemore-Adisa isn't 'well enough.' She could be dying. Probably is, without her meds."

"You don't know that, love."

"And you don't know that she's not. That's the most terrible part—the not knowing."

It was true. Because she couldn't know, Cleo wasn't able to quiet her mind. Every closing of the eyes brought new scenarios, each one more dire than the last. She felt like her skin was crawling, her head was swimming, and she couldn't quite take a full breath. She had even started to sweat, little beads forming along her hairline.

concern

"You seem distraught, Cleo. Perhaps a break? It's nearly six o'clock—dinner soon. And you skipped lunch."

"My brain won't let me take a break. I've tried."

"That's empathy. We've always known you've been blessed with an abundance of it. Remember when you found that dead worm in your father's grass shipment and tried to perform CPR on it?"

"I was seven."

"You were eight, and it showed your compassion. You even tried to pump all five of its hearts simultaneously—a finger for each one."

"Are you telling me not to be empathetic?"

Ms. VAIN shook her head and minimized the scribbled-on screen. "No, love. I'm telling you to be careful."

Cleo snagged her silky blanket off her chair and worried at a smooth corner with her thumbs. "That's the problem. I don't even know what to be careful of."

"Well, what *do* you know?"

Cleo draped the blanket over her head. The weight of it was comforting.

"I know that there's a way to get to Miriam."

"And how do you know that?"

"Because the drones do it. They move around out there, so there's got to be space for me to move, too."

"What else?"

"I won't be the first person to be . . ." Cleo paused, shuddering. "Out there."

"That stands to reason."

"Right? I mean, we built this place, all those years ago. People had to be outside before they could come inside."

As Cleo spoke, Ms. VAIN helpfully made a bulleted list of facts in the corner of the screen.

"And Miriam's apartment can't be *too* far away. There's an outside-outside, right? Where all the plants grow and it rains and people used to play soccer for real. So there are boundaries. I mean, how big can our building be?"

Ms. VAIN blinked. "At the time of the Great Separation, three hundred living structures were built, evenly spaced from coast to coast. Each structure has six floors. These are divided into six blocks, which are further subdivided into six sections. Each of these sections comprises two hundred sixteen units."

"That's room for a lot of people."

"Over fifty-five million across the continent, which is a relatively small percentage of the population of North America prior to influenza D. However, it was a good deal more space than the remaining uninfected could fill. According to the most up-to-date article in my database, there are a significant number of units in each structure that are uninhabited."

"Calculate the total number of units in our structure, please."

Ms. VAIN responded immediately. "There are 46,656 units per structure."

"Wow," Cleo whispered. The blanket slid off her head into a silken puddle at her side.

"And each unit is fourteen hundred square feet. Combine that with the interstitial spaces for drone movement and maintenance, and—"

"This place is huge."

Ms. VAIN nodded. "Comparatively speaking . . . yes."

Cleo exhaled and shook her arms, trying to banish more of the nervous prickles. "But," she said, as much to herself as to Ms. VAIN, "we can't worry about that yet. We don't even know how to get from one apartment to another."

Ms. VAIN held up her hands apologetically. "That I have no data on. I have worked with thousands of children since I came online, and I will admit—you are the first to consider leaving her apartment. I'm not the one to ask about the logistics of escape."

Before Cleo could respond, there was a knock at the door.

"Dinner!" her father said.

Her eyes narrowing, Cleo scooped up her scroll and looked down at Ms. VAIN.

"You might not be the one to ask," she said. "But I think I know who is . . ."

Her father had just passed the bowl of broccoli when Cleo asked, "Where did you come from?"

Mr. Porter's eyes grew wide, and he started sputtering.

"Finish chewing, dear," Cleo's mom said.

He managed to wrangle down the greens, and he thumped his fist against his chest a few times to steady himself.

"Um, Cleo . . . I think that's a better question for your mother. She's the surgeon, after all . . ."

Cleo rolled her eyes and set down her fork. "No, Dad. I already know about the human reproductive system. I mean how did *you* get *here*? To this apartment. Inside. You weren't born in our living room."

Gradually, the color returned to Mr. Porter's cheeks. "Oh. Oh! Yes, Cleo. That's true. Like you, I lived with my mother and father."

"Until?"

Cleo's mom reached out, taking Mr. Porter's hand in hers. "Until he met me in *Mingle*."

Cleo's lip curled. "*Mingle*?"

"It's a virtual meeting place, which you can't visit until you're eighteen."

"Twenty-one," Mr. Porter corrected.

"Yes, like your father says, which you can't visit until you're thirty-five."

"That's better, dear."

"Ugh," Cleo groaned. "Anyway . . ."

"Yes, anyway, we met, we fell in love, and we eventually applied to cohabitate. It took a year to get the clearance."

Mr. Porter used his free hand to slap the table. "Goodness, honey—remember the medical checks?"

"So many checks!" Dr. Porter agreed. "Not a case of

influenza D reported in decades, and we still had to provide six months' worth of weekly blood tests."

"She was worth it, though."

Dr. Porter batted her eyelashes at her husband. "*You* were worth it!"

Cleo cringed. She was starting to think this wasn't worth it. "Okay, so you passed the tests, and . . . ?"

Mr. Porter took a sip of water, then licked the drops from his mustache. "And we got delivered here."

"I'd never been so nervous in my entire life," Dr. Porter admitted. "Even though we'd known each other for years . . . I'd never actually met your father."

Cleo put her fork down. "Go back to being delivered here?"

Dr. Porter smiled. "That was the fun part."

Mr. Porter chuckled, "One of the fun parts."

His wife shot him a look. "Yes. We were delivered. A drone brought a sterile pod to my apartment. I got in, closed it up, and listened to music while they flew me here. No risk of contamination."

Wrinkling her nose, Cleo asked, "Through the tube?"

Dr. Porter chuckled. "Can you imagine your father fitting through there?"

"Come here, Cleo," Mr. Porter said, and he pushed up from the table. He walked across the kitchen to their tube. Cleo followed. "See this?"

Running his fingers along the place where the tube joined the wall, Mr. Porter outlined a nearly invisible oval, like a seam between the glass of the tube itself and the stronger composite of the wall. "This is where our tube was installed. Before it was here, though, there was just a hole. Once our apartment was activated—power to the systems, climate-controlled, antiseptic sealants in place—this was the last part to close. They slid our pods in, installed the tube, and that was that."

Cleo peered at the tube. As she did, the hairs on the back of her neck stood. Hundreds of times she had watched things come in through that shuttered hole in the wall, wondering and delighting at how they'd gotten in. Not once had she considered how something might get out.

At least, not until now.

Her father interrupted her thoughts with a hand on her shoulder. Cleo was so tense she hopped.

"Why so curious, by the way?" he asked. Her teeth clenched, and she looked up at him through the veil of her curls. Sensing her discomfort, he nudged her. "Did our Cleo maybe . . . meet someone on the Green? Is that what your ten-minute study break this afternoon was for?"

Cleo's hands balled into fists so tight her fingernails stung her palms.

"No!" she hissed. "Seriously, Dad. No!"

At least she didn't have to lie.

"Bowman," her mother scolded. "You let her go on the sim? You know she's supposed to be concentrating on her test." Turning to Cleo, she wagged a broccoli-capped fork in her direction. "And you don't have time for distractions. The clock is ticking."

"I know, Mom. Believe me. It's all I can think about," she replied.

Another not-lie.

"So what did you study today?" Mr. Porter asked after finishing his sweet potato.

Cleo jabbed her fork into her own food. "Skull sutures. The displacement of synovial fluids in hyperextension. Cerebral edemas . . ."

Dr. Porter narrowed her eyes. "Brain swelling?"

"Yeah. The medicine we got in that package is for—"

"Oh yes!" Mr. Porter exclaimed. "How did that go? Find anything out?"

"Some stuff," Cleo replied, shifting in her seat.

"Such as?"

Cleo leaned forward. After one more bite of broccoli, she launched into everything she had gone over with Ms. VAIN about the medicine—how it worked, what symptoms it addressed, and how critical it was for a patient's survival. She gestured wildly, bounced in her chair, and even used her fork to draw the chemical structure of calotexina florinase on her plate. By the time she was done, she was out of breath, and she had mixed her food into a strange, squishy salad. She looked up, expecting her parents to share her grim expression. But her scowl only deepened when she saw that her mother was applauding and her dad's eyes were glazed over.

"So many great facts there, Cleo!" her mom said.

"But none of them gets the medicine where it needs to be!" Cleo lamented.

"Think of all you've learned, though."

"I don't want to think of what I've learned. I want to help her!" Cleo yelled, and she slammed her fork down so hard that sweet potato spattered across the tablecloth.

"Cleo!" her mother exclaimed.

"Calm down, honey," her father added.

"I can't! We're sitting here having dinner while Miriam Wendemore-Adisa is dying, and you're acting like it's totally fine!"

While Cleo stared at them, her nostrils flaring, Dr. Porter and her husband shared a long glance. Then her mother reached out and took her hand. Cleo tried to pull away, but Dr. Porter's grip was firm.

"Cleo, can I talk to you, surgeon to surgeon?"

Cleo blinked back a few angry tears and nodded.

"What you're feeling? It's one of the hardest parts of what we do—the realization that we can't save everyone."

"But Miriam—"

"May be beyond our help. And I know that can seem heartbreaking. But we can't let it distract us from what is here, and what is under our control. My patients. Your father's program. Your test."

"There's really *nothing* we can do?"

"We can use this moment just like you have. Study it. Be thankful for the opportunity to grow, so that what you've learned from this frustration helps another patient down the line."

Cleo shot up, ripping her hand from her mother's grasp. "That's not enough!"

Dr. Porter pressed her palms to the tabletop. "It's going to have to be, Cleo."

Cleo opened her mouth to shout back, but her mother's face was so grave that she lost the words. Instead, she spun away from the table and stomped out of the kitchen, ignoring her father's gasp and her mother's stern calls. She ran down the hall to her room and slammed the door, then threw herself on the bed and buried her head beneath a pillow to stifle her screams. As loud as she was, though, she couldn't drown out the echoes of her mother's voice.

Nothing we can do but learn.

She's beyond our help.

Beyond us.

"No!" Cleo growled, gritting her teeth to banish the terrible images that flooded her thoughts. "That *can't* be. She's wrong!"

As she lay there in the dark, though, replaying her argument with her parents in her mind, Cleo realized her mother had been right about one thing: their tube. Mr. Porter never could have fit through that little hole. He would have had to have been half his size.

Or, in other words, about as big as Cleo.

realization/decision

C leo sat curled in the corner of their kitchen, her sturdy dancer's legs pulled up tight to her body, chin on her knees. The only light in the room came from Ms. VAIN, who lay flat at her feet. Next to her was a pillowcase, all lumpy and misshapen from the objects she had shoved inside. Ms. VAIN had praised her for some of them: a change of clothes, her silky blanket, apples, a little first aid kit, a water bottle, and, of course, the medicine. She had tried to persuade Cleo that other items weren't necessary, like the skull from her model of the skeleton. But Cleo had insisted—it had felt important. Maybe she could tell her mom she was studying while on the trip?

Her parents had gone to bed hours ago, after a dozen unsuccessful tries to get Cleo to open her door. Cleo had tried to fall asleep, too—one last, desperate attempt to stop worrying. She had hoped that she would drift off, dream nothing worth remembering, and then wake up thoroughly convinced that her plan had been utterly silly and that Miriam Wendemore-Adisa would be just fine without her. But sleep didn't come. The covers got heavier and hotter, her skin got colder and sweatier, and the silence got louder and louder. Finally, she bolted upright, snapped open her scroll, and got packing. Then she tiptoed into the hallway.

Cleo spent much of her days alone—or at least, alone-ish. She had Ms. VAIN, and her parents were never more than a door away. She was used to it. But there was something different about things when her parents were asleep. Creeping past their bedroom had been agonizing: everything seemed so still, and so dark, and so electric. There were a thousand sounds she had never heard before, a million shadows she never realized were there. She decided quickly that she did not like being awake when her parents were not. It was an irrational time. An enchanted time.

A guilty time.

Twice she had frozen there, mouthing words she dared not say. Apologies. Curses. Ultimatums. What if she burst in, woke them, and declared her intent to squeeze through the tube and into the beyond? Would they understand? Would they help her?

Not likely.

In fact, Cleo thought, she'd probably end up grounded, tearing her hair out with worry for Miriam while the test loomed ever larger. She'd fail it, her mother would be furious, and Miriam would die. A spiral of consequences.

So she had pressed on.

Now, though, just fifty feet from their door, arms wrapped around her shivering legs and pounding heart, a new fear had crept in: What if she actually got out?

And what if she couldn't get back?

"Ms. VAIN?" Cleo whispered.

"Yes, love?" her teacher replied—or attempted to, at any rate. Cleo had muted her after Ms. VAIN had spent twenty minutes trying to convince her not to go. Turning the volume up to 5 percent, Cleo whispered, "In all those stories . . . did anyone ever make it home again?"

"Many do, dear," Ms. VAIN responded reassuringly. "Some left trails of pebbles or bread crumbs. Some tied strings to the beginnings of labyrinths. Some retraced their paths through wardrobes. And some liked so much where they went that they made new homes there."

"I don't have any bread crumbs."

"You have me. I'm happy to record our journey so you can retrace your steps."

Cleo sniffled. "Thank you, Ms. VAIN."

"Are you worried about your safety? Getting sick, perhaps?"

Cleo shook her head. "I read the pathogen histories, remember? No. I'm not worried about sickness in the building. At least, not my own."

They sat in silence for a good while after. Ms. VAIN

even reached into her desk and took out some cards to play solitaire. Cleo strained to hear the flipping of the cards, but with the volume so low, nothing registered.

"Love," Ms. VAIN said at last, "there is no shame in admitting that a task might be too great for you."

Cleo caught the corner of her lips between her teeth. It was hard to breathe.

"It's a simple truth, really: for all your wonderful facts, Cleo, there are a great many things about our world you do not know."

Giving herself one last chance, Cleo closed her eyes.

There was Miriam Wendemore-Adisa.

Faceless.

Helpless.

Dying.

"I know to care," she whispered, "and that's enough."

"Cleo, I—"

"Shh!" Cleo hissed. From her position, she could see the outline of her parents' door. A light had just flickered around the seal.

One of them was awake.

Cleo's knees popped, she'd stood up so quickly. Grabbing the pillowcase and her scroll, she scrambled over to the tube and slid back its cover. She shoved her things in, all the way up against the shuttered hole. Then she clambered in after them and closed the hatch.

It was tight. Very tight. Cleo had to lie on her back, her head pressed against the pillowcase and the glass of the tube cold against her nose. Her breath, which came in rapid, noisy puffs, fogged the glass.

"Ms. VAIN?" Cleo gasped.

"I'm here, love," came the response from behind her hair.

"I'm . . . I'm going to push," Cleo declared. Her teeth were chattering.

"Okay," Ms. VAIN responded.

Working her hands up past her ribs, past her scapulae, and past her cheeks, Cleo pressed against the pillowcase. Her elbows bumped the glass above her as she thrust her makeshift bag against the shutter. At first, it didn't budge, but Cleo gave it a desperate heave, and quite suddenly, it tumbled through.

Gone.

Cleo froze that way, her hands above her. She had felt the opening. Her fingers had even gone through it, briefly. They had been *out*. Just as she was about to be.

Panic seized her then—a desperate, overwhelming desire to move. She pushed again at the shutter, forcing it open. A blast of lukewarm air stirred her hair, and she heard a low hum, like someone had plucked a taut rubber band and the sound had lingered. Grasping the lip of the hole with her fingers, Cleo pulled herself back, her feet kicking and squeaking along the glass. She writhed, she wriggled, and she ripped herself through.

And, just like that, Cleo disappeared, too.

CHAPTER ELEVEN

Cleo didn't expect to fall, so when she tumbled through the hole, she couldn't help but scream. And when she landed just a few feet below, her back slammed against a metal grate with an echoing *clang*. Her whole body shaking, she jerked herself up into a crouch, arms shooting out to grab her pillowcase and scroll. Then she scuttled up against the wall, clutching her things and shivering.

Lights seemed to swim around her, green and red and orange. Her heart beat so hard and so fast that her chest hurt. Over that hum, which was much louder now, Cleo could hear a rapid, high-pitched yip. A wave of nausea struck her, and when she covered her hand with her mouth, the yipping stopped. She realized what it was: her own breath.

She was hyperventilating.

A dozen diagrams jumped into her mind, pictures of

lungs and veins and molecules. It was all jumbled, though. She remembered there were steps, ways to stop the tingling in her lips and fingers, ways to counteract the sick feeling and the fear. Something about breathing in, or breathing out . . .

Or breathing in what you breathe out.

Eyes wide, Cleo shoved her head into her pillowcase. It was still full, but there was enough room for her to fit her face into a little hollow. Inadequate spasms of air tried to fill the space, only to be dragged back into her body by the gasps she couldn't seem to stop. Unable to catch herself, she listed to the side, collapsing against the grating and curling into a ball.

It was the most afraid and miserable she'd ever been.

But she had done it. She was out.

And she had survived.

Gradually, her wind came back to her, and she found she could take steadily deeper breaths. *Carbon dioxide balance,* she thought. *Breathe in what you breathe out.*

"Cleo? Are you there?" Ms. VAIN called. Her voice was tiny—still at 5 percent.

"Y-yes," she managed. Her throat hurt, and she tasted blood—she must have bitten her tongue when she landed. She ran it over her teeth, using their ridges to find the sore spot. It stung but wasn't bad. Slowly, she pulled her head out from the pillowcase.

The first thing she saw was the steel of the grating that held her. It was thick. Solid. Meant, she decided, for people to stand on. She slid her fingers through the openings and pushed herself up a bit. The metal was cold—in fact, the air itself was chilly, with a steady current that played with her curls. Cleo tried to focus on what was beneath her, looking through the grating instead of at it, but it was dark below.

It wasn't dark everywhere, however, and as she sat up fully and took in her surroundings, her jaw dropped.

She was in a hallway. It extended farther than she could see to the left and right, and the floor seemed to be made entirely of the same stuff she sat on. The ceiling was quite high, but she could still see it, thanks to the lights. There were clusters of three bulbs at regular intervals, each one casting its own color. In every cluster, the first bulb shone green, the second red, and the third orange. When she looked right at them, Cleo could see each color perfectly well, but they mixed to give everything else a glowy sort of brown tint, including her pillowcase.

Directly across from her, there were more bulbs mounted in the wall, just above a shuttered circular hatch. There were six of them, set in a neat line. The first three matched those on the ceiling: green, red, orange. The second half went blue, red, and yellow. Farther down the hall to her left, Cleo could see another hatch, with another set of lights. She squinted to figure out if the colors were the same, but something moved in to block her view.

Something big.

Cleo threw her hands over her mouth to keep from screaming again, and she wedged herself into as small a shape as she could, pulling her pillowcase in like a shield. The thing floated by her, like a bloated bumblebee buzzing lazily through the air. Six eyes defined its face, capturing the light in their glossy black curves. The electric hum was so loud now that Cleo could feel it in her chest, and it was easy to tell its source. Four powerful rotors churned beneath the thing, keeping its buggish body aloft. It passed her by without erring from its course, and after a few moments, it disappeared from view, the hum fading along with it.

When it was gone, Cleo dared to stretch out her limbs again, and she grabbed for her scroll. Ms. VAIN took quick stock of her.

"Cleo, love, your heart rate is high, you're shivering, and your pupils are dilated. I fear you may be suffering a panic attack."

"I . . . I think I'm okay now," she replied. Her tongue felt scratchy and heavy—she had been gasping again, and she forced herself to breathe evenly through her nose.

"You saw the transport drone, yes?" Ms. VAIN said, and she displayed a three-dimensional model of the thing that had just flown past.

Cleo nodded. "I didn't know they were so big!"

"They get bigger, too," Ms. VAIN noted. "The database has designs for ones that are three times that size. Would you like to hear a story about the development of drone technology?"

"Ms. VAIN, I'm *out*," Cleo murmured.

"And you're still Cleo. And I'm still your teacher."

Cleo smiled softly. "I'm going to try to stand up now, Ms. VAIN."

"Careful, dear."

Cleo was. She pressed a hand to the wall and used it to steady herself. The grating bit into the thin rubber soles of her slippers, but it wasn't too uncomfortable. When it seemed as though her shaky legs would hold, she sighed with relief.

"Look behind you, Cleo," Ms. VAIN said softly.

Turning, Cleo realized she was staring at her family's unit. Part of the shutter hung loosely from its hinge. She reached up and touched it. It fell off, hitting the grating with a sharp *ping*.

"That's not good . . . ," Cleo said.

"I suppose it'd be easy to crawl back in."

"We have to find Ms. Wendemore-Adisa's apartment first," Cleo insisted. "But I guess it's too much to ask that she be our neighbor."

Ms. VAIN smiled. "One way to find out. 631445."

"Right," Cleo said, and she scanned the outside wall of her unit, looking for her own familiar numbers. There were none, though—just more of those colored lightbulbs above her hatch: green, red, orange, orange, violet, yellow.

"Six bulbs. Six numbers," Cleo murmured.

"It makes sense," Ms. VAIN replied, and she brought up the schematics of the transport drone again. "See those lenses?"

"You mean its eyes?"

"That's not a bad analogy, love. According to the design, those are frequency receptors."

"So the drones are just following the colored lights?"

Ms. VAIN beamed. "Precisely! Of course, the colors are your brain's way of reading those frequencies. Really, it's just different wavelengths of light energy, and that's what the drone is searching for—a specific pattern of wavelengths."

"And this is my unit's pattern," Cleo said, running her hand along the bulbs. They were warm to the touch. "The first three match the bulbs on the ceiling, and on the unit across the hall."

"What about the patterns down the hall?" Ms. VAIN prodded.

Cleo took a deep breath, even though her lungs were a bit achy still. She gathered up her pillowcase and slung it over her shoulder. Then she took Ms. VAIN and started walking. Her footsteps pinged softly against the grate, and Cleo couldn't help but look back at her hatch, and her colors. She did so five times, even though the additional hatches on her side were only a few hundred feet away.

"Green, red, orange, orange, violet, green," she noted. "Only one is different from ours."

"That makes sense."

Cleo nodded and said, "Notepad."

Ms. VAIN complied, and Cleo sat down to do some calculations. As she worked, two more transport drones drifted by. The first looked identical to the last one she'd seen, but the second was different. For starters, it flew in the opposite direction. It also flew higher—near the ceiling, in fact, and much higher than Cleo could reach, even by jumping. The biggest difference, though, was its back half. Rather than looking like the heavy abdomen of a bug, it was just rails. It had dropped off its delivery, Cleo supposed.

"Any luck with the numbers, love?"

Cleo's face scrunched in thought. "I think so," she said after several more swipes of her finger. "If our unit is 412263, then this one is probably 412262 or 412264. That would account for the last light being a different color."

"Stands to reason."

"And if the numbers match up with the colors, that means that this one is definitely 412264, since it starts and ends with the same color, which would be four."

Cleo drew a little chart of numbers. Her handwriting was sloppy, since her hands were still shaking, but Ms. VAIN fixed her letters so that they were printed perfectly.

"If all this is right, then one equals red."

"That is the lowest frequency color of the visible spectrum," Ms. VAIN noted helpfully.

"And two is orange. Three is yellow, four is green. The blue across the hall—a five, maybe? Six is purple."

"If it's of interest, this matches the colors of the rainbow."

Cleo suddenly remembered. "Roy G. Biv?"

Ms. VAIN grinned. "Just so, love. I taught you that lesson back when we first studied the retina. I'm honored that you remember."

colored lights

code

Cleo said the letters out loud again, one by one. "There's seven of them, though."

"That's a bit misleading. The 'I,' for 'indigo,' was a hotly debated color for many, many years. The frequencies it tends to fall between are indistinguishable from blue—at least, by the human eye. ROYGBIV as a mnemonic is easier to say with a vowel between the 'B' and 'V,' though, so the color stayed."

"So when they built this system . . ."

"They probably wanted clearly defined frequencies. Thus, no indigo."

Cleo peered down the dim passage. "We won't know for sure until we find a five in order . . . a blue on our side of the hallway."

"Shall we keep going, then?"

Cleo nodded, and they slipped farther down the hall. The gentle breeze seemed slightly stronger here, though nothing else changed: the walls were still made of a smooth, muted brown plastic, the lights in the ceiling were still green, red, and orange, and the occasional transport drone cruised by. Sure enough, the bulb sequence for the next unit ended with a blue. Cleo tapped at it, glad that it confirmed their theory, but her mind was already somewhere else.

"If the next one ends in purple . . ."

"Violet," Ms. VAIN corrected.

"Yes, violet . . . then what's after that?"

Ms. VAIN blinked, helpfully preparing a list of the ten most probable answers, but Cleo was already walking, the pillowcase bouncing on her shoulder and Ms. VAIN swinging at her side. She passed the next unit and its final, violet bulb.

Then she froze.

They had reached an intersection. The hallway spilled out into a much wider space, and the grating continued both to the left and right. In the middle, however, it seemed to fall away, leaving a shadowy, yawning hole. Both above her and to either side, transport drones hummed along. Cleo marveled as another seemed to rise out of the floor, its spinning rotors lifting it. It continued straight upward, and as she followed its path, Cleo realized there was an opening in the ceiling as well. The grating formed a sort of ledge around the hole in the floor, and she crept toward its lip to look down.

"Careful, love . . . ," Ms. VAIN warned. "There's no guardrail . . ."

"I just need to see . . ."

And then she did. In the space below, the hallways continued, just like they did on her level. The lights, however, were different. Daring to turn her gaze upward, Cleo saw that it was the same above. Instead of a green-red-orange cluster on the ceiling, the sequence began with blue.

"Ms. VAIN!" Cleo shouted, "The first color! I think it tells you the floor! All the lights down here start with green, but up there—"

Cleo was interrupted in terrifying fashion. A sudden blast of air from below knocked her back just as a blinding white light flashed. She landed on her rear on the grating, and a steely shiver echoed through the metal. When she could see again, she covered her face with her arms and screamed.

Three drones hovered above the hole. They were smaller than the transport kind, but even more insect-like. Powerful lamps attached to the front and back of each banished the brownish hue of the hallway, and their rotors flared to either side like the wings of a dragon-fly. Dangling from beneath their spherical bodies were what Cleo initially mistook for legs. However, as they flew directly over her, she realized that they were actually tools: rotary saws, welding torches, screwdrivers, even a gleaming drill bit. She stayed flat against the grate until they were well past her, and then she scrambled up to watch them go.

"Ms. VAIN?"

"Repair drones, dear," came the reply once Cleo had picked up her scroll.

Fascinated, and with her heart still thumping, Cleo followed the trio of drones back down her own hallway. Her eyes widened when she saw where they had stopped.

Her unit.

"What are they . . . ," she began, but their intent became clear almost immediately. One used a leg like a pair of pliers, picking up the broken piece of shutter. It flew upward until it had the plate level with her tube. The other two drones extended their own legs, and a flash of blue flame sent sparks cascading down through the openings in the floor, showering in light the network of pipes and wires that had been hidden before. In a matter of moments, they had sealed the shutter closed, and they flew off as quickly as they had arrived. Cleo dashed forward to look.

It was completely repaired, as if she had never escaped at all.

Cautiously, Cleo reached up. She couldn't even get her hand close before the lingering heat from the welding forced her back.

I'm locked out, she thought.

Another surge of panic bubbled inside her.

"Ms. VAIN . . . Ms. VAIN, they closed it! They closed the hatch! What do we do?"

"Sit, love. And breathe. Just breathe."

Cleo collapsed beneath her shutter. She turned Ms. VAIN to face her, and the first of Cleo's tears pattered against the screen.

"There, there," Ms. VAIN comforted. "It'll be all right, Cleo."

"I . . . I yelled at them! And I didn't say goodbye! What if I never see them again? What if I can't get back?"

"Think, dear. Packages get in all the time. That's how we'll get into Miriam's unit, and that's how we'll get home again. Just wait for a delivery."

"Okay . . . ," Cleo sobbed. "Okay . . ."

Even with Ms. VAIN's soothing words, it took Cleo a long time to calm down. Eventually, she grabbed the hem of her shirt and used it to wipe her eyes. After another ragged, lung-rattling breath, she said, "I feel like I've lived a year in the past ten minutes."

Ms. VAIN chuckled. "This is more excitement than most of my students experience in five years. Kind of makes you wish for the relaxing calm of studying for the biggest test of your life, doesn't it?"

Cleo tried to laugh, but it came out as a snort.

"Ugh, I'm a mess."

"You're exhausted, love. Remember, it's three-thirty in the morning."

"But Miriam Wendemore-Adisa could still be so far away!"

"You've already taken the first step to finding her, though."

Cleo looked down the hall. "It was a big step, too."

"The biggest you've ever taken."

Cleo shivered. Reaching into her pillowcase, she pulled out the skull, her apples, and her water bottle. Beneath, still folded up tight, was her silky blanket. As she wrapped it around herself, she murmured, "Difficulty thinking, dry lips, mood swings, heart palpitations."

Ms. VAIN nodded. "Yes, those are the symptoms of exhaustion."

"Then I think I'm exhausted."

"Told you so."

"You did . . . ," Cleo grumbled, and her eyes closed. For the first time since the medicine arrived, she imagined nothing at all.

CHAPTER TWELVE

Cleo awoke to a high-pitched noise. She sat up slowly, rubbing at the sleep crust around her eyes before opening them. When she did, she was startled to see a pair of glasses staring back at her. Or, at least, that was what she thought at first. As her vision adjusted to the light, she recognized it as another drone.

"You're so tiny!" Cleo said. The drone just hovered there. Besides the two huge lenses on its front, it had a little domed body, no bigger than Cleo's fist. Most of that had to be its flying mechanism, she guessed. Altogether, it reminded her of a very large ladybug, though she couldn't really tell what color it was. Everything except the bulbs in the hallway looked brown.

"Do you have someplace to be? A job?" Cleo asked it. Other than the whine of its motor, it didn't respond. Curious, she reached up, offering her palm. The drone settled on it, and the whining stopped.

"So light, too . . . Ms. VAIN, what is this little one?"

There was no response. Cleo saw her scroll, open and dark, a few feet away. To the drone, or perhaps to nobody in particular, she said, "She must have powered down to save charge."

Lifting her arm, Cleo encouraged the drone to take flight again. To her surprise, it tumbled from her hand, landing on the grating with a plasticky *thunk*. It clicked a few times, its motor sputtered, and then it rose in the air, swinging back and forth as it recalibrated.

"Silly thing . . . ," Cleo muttered, and she tapped her scroll to unlock the screen.

"Good morning, Cleo!" Ms. VAIN said cheerily. "It's nine forty-three. Have you been asleep this whole time?"

Cleo stretched her legs out, pointing her toes and then curling them until they cracked satisfyingly. "I think so. We have a curious visitor," she said, and she turned the screen to face the little drone.

"According to the database, that's an observation drone."

"What does it do?"

"The name says it all. It just observes. Sometimes, people can log in to the network and see what they see."

"Does that mean there's someone actually looking at me right now?"

"The chances of that are quite slim. There are thousands upon thousands of these in the structure. The usage data suggests that only two or three are ever patched into, and that's mostly to keep track of repairs. Their standard programming is to fly patrol routes and look for anomalies. This might even be the drone that identified your broken shutter."

"Hey," Cleo said. "Did you snitch on me, little one?"

It didn't reply.

"If the hatch is fixed, why is it still here?"

Ms. VAIN chuckled. "Well, I reckon it fancies you an anomaly, love."

Cleo tensed. "Um . . . they're not going to try to 'repair' me, are they?"

Ms. VAIN blinked. "I'm sorry. There's no record in the database of how an observer drone might regard a human. You may be the first it ever encountered."

"Maybe we should get moving, then, before it decides what to make of me."

With one eye on the tiny drone, Cleo bundled up her things and started down the passage toward the hole. She held Ms. VAIN before her, facing out so she could see, too. She didn't get very far, before the observer drone whined its way in front of her. It seemed to be staring at her, those two big lenses reflecting Cleo's own face as it bobbed up and down in the air.

"Excuse us," Cleo said, and she set down Ms. VAIN. Then she reached up to gently nudge the drone to the side. It apparently thought she meant to hold it again, because it tried to land on her hand. It missed, though, and once more tumbled to the grating.

"Clumsy widget," Cleo murmured as she picked it up.

After a few seconds, its metallic squeal began again, and it took off, zipping around her head like one of the flies in the simulator. Cleo wrinkled her nose.

"Something the matter, dear?" Ms. VAIN asked.

"I think it means to follow us."

"Makes sense. That's its job."

"But that noise ..."

"Would you like me to suggest a few solutions?"

Cleo nodded.

"The fastest, most permanent fix would be to destroy the drone."

Cleo gasped. "No!"

"It is not a living thing, Cleo."

"But look at his little face!"

"It's a he now?"

Cleo shrugged. "Elly the Elephant is a she. Silky Blanket is a she. Dad calls the simulator a he. Mom named her tea mug Vanessa."

"I see your point. Still, as a fellow program housed in an inanimate interface machine, I can assure you that it—"

"He."

"That *he* will feel no pain."

"Not a chance."

"In that case, you could find a way to trap him here."

Cleo looked around. There wasn't much to use. She even peered through the grating, asking Ms. VAIN to increase her screen to full brightness so Cleo could see below. But there wasn't a way to use the grating like a cage—no hinges

cares about the drone (handwritten annotation)

or bigger openings she could find. Just a bunch of pipes for what she assumed were compost and waste removal, and cables for electricity to each unit.

"Maybe he'll get bored and go away on his own?"

He didn't. Cleo made it all the way to the intersection, and the observer drone followed her each step of the way. Every so often, it would circle her, and every time she tried to swat it away, it attempted to land on her. The worst part was the noise—even at the intersection, which was much, much busier than it had been in the middle of the night, Cleo could clearly hear the little drone's buzzing.

"That's going to drive me mad," she declared as she slumped against the wall.

"Still think he's cute?" Ms. VAIN teased.

"Yes," Cleo replied defiantly. "Cute, but obnoxious. I was trying to think of what Miriam Wendemore-Adisa's address colors would be, and I couldn't even concentrate for half a second."

"If the pattern holds, her unit would be violet-yellow-red-green-green-blue."

Cleo looked up through the wide hole. There was a line of transport drones steadily ascending through the right side, while dozens of empty drones slowly drifted downward on the left. It was like clockwork, and it reminded Cleo of something.

"It's like . . . ," she began, but before she could catch the thought, the little drone whizzed by her ear.

"That's *it*," Cleo huffed, and she reached into her bag.

She pulled out her blanket and tossed it over the drone. It wasn't heavy enough to drag the drone to the floor, but it blocked its visual sensors, and within seconds the drone crashed into the wall and fell to the ground.

Cleo hurried to the crumpled-up blanket. She spread it open gingerly, and the little drone shot out of the piled fabric like an angry hornet, buzzing around her head for a moment before settling into a hover near her ear.

"Okay, so no blanket," Cleo murmured. She shoved her hand back into her pillowcase and touched everything. Chucking an apple at it would probably feel good, but it might damage the drone, and she'd be down an apple. Pouring water over it might short it out . . . Her spare shirt would probably just have the same effect as the blanket. And the skull . . .

. . . The skull?

Cleo pulled the model from the bag, looking at it intently. There was an opening beneath the jawline up into the cranial cavity, made wider than normal so she could see the interior of the skull without breaking it. She pursed her lips, narrowed her eyes, and held out her hand.

The drone instantly alit on her palm, perching there like it owned the place. Slowly, Cleo brought the skull around. The drone didn't move. Then, in a single swoop, she brought the skull over the top of the drone. It whirred to life immediately, a jet of air blasting her hand. However, instead of taking off, the little thing trapped itself inside the skull. Cleo laughed triumphantly and set the skull down.

"I promise, little guy, that when I come back, I'll let you out."

The drone rattled around in the skull, but there wasn't much space to maneuver. Cleo couldn't even hear its whine. She sighed with relief and stood up to go.

"See, Ms. VAIN?" she said smugly, "I told you that skull would come in handy."

Ms. VAIN arched an eyebrow. "Um, Cleo?"

"Yes?"

"Turn around."

Inches from her face was the skull. Cleo stumbled back a few steps, a hand over her suddenly leaping heart. The little drone hovered there, its lenses pushed up against the eye sockets of the skull and its rotors thrust through the opening at the base.

"Seriously?" Cleo muttered. In response, the rotors tilted and the skull puttered forward slowly, the jaw hanging open in a perpetual laugh. Cleo couldn't help but snicker, too. "Not so fast now, are we?" she teased.

"And much quieter, too," Ms. VAIN observed.

"Thank goodness for that."

As Cleo watched, the drone seemed to experiment with its new shell. It flew around in a lazy loop and then spun itself in the air. It went too quickly, though, and the tiny thing got twisted inside the skull. Cleo winced as it took off again . . .

. . . and collided with the wall again. Unlike the first time, though, it didn't fall. Instead, it swiveled until the drone's lenses lined up with the sockets once more.

"Seems you've got a suit of armor!" Cleo said.

The skull smiled in reply.

With the noise back to a manageable hum, Cleo found herself able to think. "We need a way up," she concluded after a few moments. "If our floor is green, and the one above us is blue, that means violet—Miriam's floor—should be two above us. But I don't see a staircase or a ladder or an elevator anywhere."

"Well, we have only explored a very small part of a very big building," Ms. VAIN noted.

"Right. So . . . onward?"

"I'm recording," Ms. VAIN assured her.

CHAPTER THIRTEEN

With her left hand touching the wall, it took Cleo ten minutes to circle the block that her unit was in. The grated floor was a constant, as were the lines of transport drones humming along. And at every corner, one of those sets of holes opened in the floor and ceiling, allowing drones to move from level to level.

"It's like the circulatory system," Cleo observed, and she took a great, drooly bite of an apple. She had plunked herself down at the same corner she had started from, peering across the way at the opposite hall, where the green-red-orange ceiling lights continued. Her floating skull companion twitched in the air, looking at the apple, then Cleo's mouth, then the apple again. She held it up, and the drone smacked into it. Cleo giggled.

"What's like the circulatory system, love?" Ms. VAIN asked.

Cleo pointed with her drippy apple hand. "The halls and the drones. See how the ones with deliveries to make stay on one side of the hole, and the empty ones keep to the other? That's like arteries and veins carrying oxygen-rich and -poor blood to and from the parts of the body. The repair drones? Those are the platelets."

"An interesting analogy!"

"It's what I was trying to think of before Skullface here interrupted us."

"You're calling him Skullface?"

Cleo took another bite of apple and chewed thoughtfully. "No, you're right. He needs a better name."

"Would you like to hear a story about a skull with a name?"

Cleo arched an eyebrow. "There can't be too many of those . . ."

"I have 3,941 named skulls in the database."

"I suppose all skulls had names, once. But that's sort of like my toenails each being named Cleo," she said, wriggling her toes in her slippers.

"These are skulls who are specifically referred to by name as skulls, rather than as parts of the humans to which they formerly belonged."

"Wow," Cleo muttered. She waved the apple at the little drone. "You've got competition!"

"Probably the most famous—that is, the one most frequently referenced in a variety of media, including print and film—is from William Shakespeare's *Hamlet*."

"Was it a boy skull or a girl skull?"

"The owner of the skull had been a man: 'a fellow of infinite jest, of most excellent fancy.'"

Cleo looked up at the smiling jaw and the googly lenses peering out.

"Yep. That's him, all right. What was the name?"

"Yorick."

"Was that the man's name, or the skull's name?"

"Both."

"See? Like toenails," Cleo observed, and she solemnly raised her apple. Then she touched the skull on the crown. "I hereby dub thee Yorick," she proclaimed.

The drone just stared at her.

"Now, Yorick, my good man! Mayhap you can show a maiden fair to the nearest staircase, ladder, elevator, or trampoline?" *creative/funny*

"Trampoline, dear?"

"Yeah. We've got to get up there somehow . . ."

"Where on earth would you have encountered a trampoline?"

"Simulator. Tessa had one for her tenth birthday party. It was kind of boring, though—basically just 'breeze down, breeze up' while you bent your knees. The merry-go-round was more fun."

"I recall you getting ill after Tessa's party."

"I did! My first case of motion sickness. It was fascinating! I actually got to feel the cake come up my trachea! Some got stuck in my sinuses, though . . . that wasn't so great."

"I imagine not."

Cleo glanced at her apple. For some reason, she wasn't hungry anymore. Still, she clamped it between her teeth, sucking on the juices that streamed out while she picked up her pillowcase and Ms. VAIN. From the looks of things, there wasn't much of a difference between the four directions at the intersection, except that she knew exactly what was behind her—home. And based on the numbers, in addition to going up two floors, she needed to find an entirely new section in an entirely new block.

So she had some walking to do in any case.

The trouble was, she wasn't sure which way was up, numerically speaking. She tried to read the ceiling lights in the distance, but it all became a muddled brown after about five hundred feet. So she shrugged and just started walking in a straight line, past the hole, past dozens of utterly aloof transport drones, and past banks of unblinking lights.

She walked for an hour.

And everything looked the same.

Well, not exactly the same—the lights did continue their familiar pattern. It was a bit mesmerizing, actually. Cleo found herself thinking, *Just one more set, one more hall, one more green in the fourth position.* And when something big happened, like entering a new block, where the ceiling lights changed? That was cause for a little cheer. Still, all that walking, and no way up.

"We're getting nowhere, Yorick," Cleo moaned. "Except farther and farther from home."

Yorick responded by bonking into the wall.

"Silly drone." Cleo smirked and reached out to pat him on the parietal bone. To her surprise, Yorick managed to hold the weight of her hand and the skull. She could hear his rotors whir, straining against the pressure. Sure, he eventually sank, but he seemed a lot stronger than Cleo had given him credit for.

At the same time, another transport drone, its beetle-like cylindrical shell domed and shining, lumbered past. Cleo watched it meander its way to the next intersection, glide above the hole, and then effortlessly ascend. She pursed her lips.

"Ms. VAIN, is there any information in the database about how much weight a transport drone can carry?"

Ms. VAIN blinked. "Depending on the classification of drone, they can fly payloads of up to four hundred pounds."

"And what if that weight suddenly changed? What would one do?"

"There is no information on that topic," Ms. VAIN said, and she leaned forward at her desk. "Why do you ask?"

Cleo set Ms. VAIN down and rubbed her suddenly sweaty palms against her pants. "I'm scheming," she replied.

"Would you like to hear a story about a girl who attempts to ride a flying creature? The protagonists survive in slightly over fifty-nine percent of the narratives!"

Cleo shot her teacher a look. "Are you being sarcastic?"

"No; encouraging, always. I've had over twenty million hours of conversations with children your age, and in that time I've been able to observe twelve-year-olds' reactions to survival and death rates. They tend to be more receptive to information when it is couched positively. Would you have preferred that I tell you that the stories indicate a forty-one percent chance of death?"

"Fair point," Cleo muttered.

"And in any event, I'm not able to deduce which of the thousands of tales would be most applicable, since many of the things being ridden are of a fanciful nature. Would you consider a dragon a reasonable analogue for a transport drone? Or perhaps a pegasus? Maybe a flying carpet? I have several wherein a woman utilizes an umbrella, but it isn't clear whether the umbrella is the mode of transportation or simply a way for her to stay dry and shaded as she transports herself."

Cleo shrugged. "I don't know if a story is going to help me here, but I appreciate the encouragement anyway."

"My pleasure, love. I'm certain you have a chance to be successful."

Exhaling slowly, Cleo began measuring up the transport drones that passed. She dismissed the empty ones immediately; she had only ever seen them go down through the holes. The biggest of those with packages to deliver would have to do. At least, she thought, she'd have plenty of time in the hallway to jump on the slow-moving things before they reached the hole.

With a "Wish me luck," Cleo closed her scroll. She tucked it into the pillowcase, and then she knotted the top. Holding it tightly in her left hand, she sized up the next transport drone. It was one of the bigger ones, all brownish head and heavy body, and it came gliding down the hall at a pace no faster than Cleo could crawl.

Cleo wasn't really sure why she felt the need to yell "Heeee-ya!" as she leaped onto the drone's back; it just sort of came out. It didn't help much, though. Before she could get a grip with her hands or thighs, she found herself slipping off the other side. She hit the grated floor with a *clang* and sat up, rubbing at her sore hip and shoulder.

Yorick hummed down next to her, smiling that toothy grin.

"Yeah, laugh it up," Cleo muttered. Yorick bobbed a bit, but said nothing.

Attempt number two went slightly better, though it was a smaller drone, and it must have been carrying close to its maximum weight, because as soon as Cleo got situated, it sank to the floor, rotors buzzing angrily. Cleo hopped off, patted it on the end beam, and whispered, "Sorry!"

It took her three more attempts, but finally she found one big enough to hold her weight, but not so big that she'd fall off, and she managed to time her jump correctly. The drone sagged beneath her but didn't stop, and she clung to its payload, cheek pressed to the cylinder and arms and legs splayed wide. The pillowcase dangled from her hand brushing along the grating below. She hoped the jostling wouldn't damage the calotexina florinase, but it was a risk she had to take.

The drone was in no hurry, so Cleo chanced a look up. The hole was about fifty feet away. Cleo could see the plodding shadows of the other drones, flowing through the passageways like blood. Sometimes they would pause, allowing another drone to pass.

"They're so polite, Yorick," she said. The skull had taken to matching her speed, and it hovered just above her. She could feel the air pushed down from its tiny rotors, and it ruffled her hair.

Once the hole came into full view, Cleo dared to flex her fingers. They cracked, and she scooted forward as much as she could; it made her a bit queasy not to be able to see exactly how close they were to the opening. That uneasy feeling intensified as they approached the yawning lip, and Cleo felt herself suddenly aware of many things: Her sweaty palms. Her precarious grip on the pillowcase. The beginnings of an ache in her thigh muscles. The looseness of her left slipper.

"Okay," she whispered. "Okayokayokay . . . don't panic. This will work. It'll work. Yorick, this is going to work, right?"

Yorick seemed not to have an opinion one way or the other. He watched, eye lenses glinting, as Cleo's drone flew over the hole. Cleo couldn't bear to look, though, and she squeezed her eyes shut tight. Through clenched teeth, she hissed, "Please work . . . please . . . please . . ."

A wash of wind surrounded Cleo, the airstream from below and above joining the cross breezes of the hallways. She could hear a low whistle, loud enough to match the whirring of the transport drone, Yorick's metallic hum, and the reedy sound of her own breathing. Her right palm, sweaty and slick, squeaked against the smoothness of the shell, and Cleo felt her whole body tense.

And then they started to rise.

But not politely.

Cleo's stomach lurched as the drone did, and the noise of its rotors chopping at the air drowned out everything else. It ascended a few feet over that void, but then, just as suddenly, sank back down, fighting to lift both its cargo and Cleo. Another drone had snuck in beneath them, and Cleo cried out as she felt the impact of her drone thunking into the one below.

Her hands slipped a few inches.

"C'mon . . . up. Up!" she shouted.

As though it heard her, the drone seemed to find another gear, its rotors growling as it tried to claw its way upward. The increase in power sent the drone surging, and the abrupt jag startled Cleo so much that her eyes flew open . . .

Just in time to see the spinning blades of another drone above her.

Cleo screamed and let go, rolling sideways right before the two transports collided. A hideous grinding screech filled the air as the blades raked the plastic dome of Cleo's drone.

Or rather, what used to be Cleo's drone.

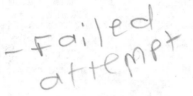

CHAPTER FOURTEEN

Cleo landed back-first on the drone beneath her, blasting all the air out of her lungs and causing the drone to list badly to the side. She felt herself slipping off, and she desperately tried to turn herself about, to grab onto anything she could, but with one hand closed like a vise around her pillowcase, she couldn't hold on.

She fell again.

Lights spun around her, and she careened off drone after drone, slamming into them without being able to get a grip. Each impact rattled her whole body, twisting her limbs about and pummeling her. Still, she reached out. She flailed and clutched at anything she could, until finally she managed to tangle her arms around one of the rails of an empty transport. Too dizzy and hurt to care that she was being carried downward, Cleo hung on for dear life.

Miserably, through tear-clouded eyes, she watched the floors rush by.

Yellow.

Then orange.

Then red.

And then into darkness.

The poor empty transport drone she had dragged with her, the one that probably saved Cleo's life, hit a hard surface with a crack of plastic and a shudder that threw Cleo off. As soon as she rolled free, the drone shot upward, disappearing almost instantly from view. Shaking and sore, Cleo curled around her pillowcase and wept.

She cried for a long time. A few of her tears were for her hurt—her legs and back were particularly battered. More of them acknowledged her own stupidity—how could she be so reckless? So bold? It had been nothing like simulator trampolines or falling out of bed or swing-abouts in her father's arms. It had been uncontrollable and chaotic and so very *fast*. Most of her tears, though, flowed when she thought of her parents. She had been wildly selfish, she now realized, thinking she could be like her mother.

Thinking she could save someone.

And now they were above her—Mom and Dad and Miriam and *everyone*—so very far up, and they were probably inconsolable with worry and grief and fear. Nobody simply disappeared.

But I am in the dark and I am alone and I have disappeared, Cleo thought, and she sobbed all the harder.

CHAPTER FIFTEEN

I t was stone-cold fear that halted Cleo's sobs. A violent
gurgle, throaty and wet and very close, forced her into
a sudden backward scramble. She kicked and screamed
until her back hit something solid, and then she curled up,
shielding her face with her arms.

Nothing happened.

Cleo tried to swallow but found it impossibly hard. She
opened her arms just a crack to peek out.

She saw only blackness.

"M–Ms. VAIN?" she whispered. "Please . . ."

But of course Ms. VAIN was rolled up inside her
pillowcase.

And she had left that where she'd fallen, near the gurgling thing.

A helpless whimper escaped her lips, and Cleo ran her
hands through her tangled curls, pulling at them, hoping

the fresh shock of pain would embolden her, or at least turn her panic into action. The gurgle rumbled again, and Cleo yelled at it, a high-pitched keen that drowned out the guttural noise. At the same time, she pulled off one of her slippers, desperately flinging it toward the sound. It was flimsy and useless, but the gurgling stopped, and it felt good to throw something, so she took off her other slipper and held it up, ready to hurl it, too.

And she did, just as a searing yellow light blinded her.

"No! No!" Cleo shrieked, and she lashed out with both hands, clawing the air with her nails, swinging wildly.

A familiar, irritating whine, quiet but persistent, slowed her fury.

"Y-Yorick?" she gasped. Hovering there, grinning, was the skull. From its eye sockets beamed twin rays of light, and as the little drone circled her, Cleo blinked away the floating black spots in her vision. Then she held out her hand, palm upward.

The skull settled there, just as primly as he pleased.

Cleo allowed herself another sob, this one of sheer relief. To Yorick's vibrating dismay, she yanked him in, hugging the skull to her chest. She could hear the tiny drone knocking about inside the cranium, but she didn't care. She needed him close.

When she was ready, she gently twisted Yorick, aiming those yellow beams out into the darkness. They fell across a concrete floor, its rough texture casting tiny shadows along the edges of the light. In the middle of the beams sat her pillowcase, saggy and forlorn. And past it, where the gurgles came from?

A massive wall of horizontal pipes.

As Cleo stared, one of those pipes obliged her with a squelching, bubbly cacophony as something jetted through the huge tube. It was made of steel, so Cleo couldn't see inside like she would've been able to with the tube in her own kitchen. Just a few seconds later, another pipe echoed the first. Cleo cringed. It was one of the more disgusting things she'd ever heard, like if someone had stuck a stethoscope to her belly during a bad stomachache.

The uneven floor cut into Cleo's palms and knees as she started to crawl forward, so she retrieved her slippers first. Standing wasn't much better, but it didn't truly hurt—or at least, it didn't hurt enough to bother her more than the pain in her shins, hips, and shoulders from her fall. With a shiver, Cleo realized just how lucky she was not to have broken any bones, and she silently thanked that empty drone for being there.

Her gratitude evaporated, though, when she got to her pillowcase.

"No . . . oh, Yorick, no!" Cleo wailed.

At first, Cleo had thought her water bottle had cracked open, because there was a slowly spreading puddle surrounding one corner of the bag. When Yorick's light shone directly on it, though, she saw the truth.

The liquid was bright blue.

Not daring to breathe, Cleo untied the knot and eased

her scroll out of the pillowcase. It, at least, seemed undamaged. Beneath, the transparent foam inside the package was crushed, a crumbly pile of it crammed into the corner of the bag. At the center of the pile were the spheres of calotexina florinase.

Or what was left of them.

With trembling fingers, Cleo picked up a scrap of one of the flimsy plastic globes. It was gooey with blue medicine, and a rivulet of it oozed down her palm. It smelled vinegary and metallic. She tossed it away and pawed through the rest of the foam. The second sphere seemed as though it had ruptured close to the first, their contents mingling and leaking all over the bottom of her bag. The third, though?

Her teeth chattering, Cleo dug out the final globe. Sodden bits of packaging clung to it, and she gingerly picked them off, wiping her fingertips on the fabric of the pillowcase after each one. More of the medicine stained her hands, but after a few moments, she sighed with relief.

The last one was unbroken.

Cradling the jewel-like sphere in her lap, Cleo emptied the contents of her pillowcase on the ground. Her water bottle was fine. Her remaining apples were as bruised as she was, but were probably still edible. And her silky blanket was spared most of the medicine, which had squished out the opposite corner. Taking a moment to nuzzle her cheek against the cool of her blanket for comfort, Cleo sniffled. Then she carefully swaddled the lone sphere in the blanket and returned it to her bag.

"Take care of it, Silky," she muttered. The noisy pipes spat and grumbled in reply.

"How did your trip go, love?" Ms. VAIN asked cheerfully when Cleo logged in.

"I messed up, Ms. VAIN. Badly," Cleo whispered.

"I can see you're upset," Ms. VAIN offered gently. "I'm listening if you want to talk."

"I fell, and . . ." Cleo paused, looking up through the hole. She could make out a bit of the brownish light above, but there was no sign of the hall lights or any of the units. "I think we're lost. But that's not the worst part."

"You're not hurt, are you, dear?"

Cleo shook her head. "No. But the medicine . . . most of it is gone. We only have one sphere left."

"Oh. Is there anything I can do?"

Cleo closed her eyes and thought. "Can you look up the standard dosage for calotexina florinase? Or, even better, how many days' worth of medicine came in each sphere?"

Ms. VAIN blinked. "It depends on the patient and her condition, but even if she took the maximum safe dosage, one sphere should last for ten days."

"So that was a month's supply," Cleo said grimly.

"Makes sense. And maybe there's a silver lining here?"

Cleo rubbed at one of the bruises on her leg. "What's that?"

"Well, it's the last week of May. Perhaps if we get the remaining sphere to Miriam Wendemore-Adisa, it will buy her enough time to order a new supply at the beginning of the month."

"I hope so," Cleo said, and she offered her teacher a wan smile. It didn't last long, though—something seemed off, more than just the frightening fall or the loss of the medicine or the eerie noises of the pipes. With so many immediate questions to answer—Where were they? Where should they go from here? How long would it take to get to Miriam now?—and a darker, scarier one hiding behind those (*Will I ever get home again?*), it was impossible for Cleo to grasp enough of that new, murky uneasiness in order to properly sit with it.

"One thing at a time, Cleo," she told herself, and she stood up.

"Sound advice, love," Ms. VAIN said.

It took exactly one try for Cleo to give up on climbing the pipes. They were far too thick and smooth to grip well, and she found herself so terrified of dropping the pillowcase that she didn't dare risk going very high in any case. So she grabbed Yorick by the jaw and slowly spun him left and right. His beams shot through the open space, revealing another long corridor. There were no telltale marks indicating where they should go; Cleo supposed it was too much to ask for a THIS WAY TO THE STAIRS sign.

After consulting with Ms. VAIN, Cleo decided to go right. Her teacher called her reasoning astute: the noise in the pipes ran from right to left, and if they were sewage or compost pipes, then they logically must have come from the units above. Since that was where Cleo desperately needed to be . . .

The rubber soles of her slippers scratched along the concrete, and Cleo found herself missing the grating. She forced herself not to think of the nice, carpeted floors of her apartment, too, because even the briefest memory of home filled her with an overwhelming urge to sit down, cover her face with her hair, and cry.

So she pressed on, trying not to think of much at all.

Eventually, a pattern emerged in the passage. Every time a hole opened in the ceiling, a series of vertical pipes came down and met with the ones that ran along the hall-way, making a series of upside-down T's. Cleo passed a dozen of them before she reached the next major intersection. She took a quick drink from her water bottle, then considered her options.

All four directions had pipes.

All four directions seemed to go on forever.

All four directions were dark.

Except for one.

"Yorick, no lights for a second," Cleo muttered, and she put a hand over the drone's beams. It took her a few moments to adjust, but when she did, she saw that there was a bit of brightness coming from the hallway opposite her. Squinting, Cleo tried to make out more. She couldn't tell precisely what color the light was—white or yellow or pale green, maybe? And she couldn't tell how far away the source was.

But she could tell that it was moving.

"Hey!" Cleo shouted suddenly.

"What is it, Cleo?" Ms. VAIN asked. Cleo held her in the same hand as the pillowcase, so all she could see was blue-stained fabric.

"I think it's ... something," Cleo replied excitedly. "Lights. Another observation drone, maybe? What if it's one of the ones a person is watching through? They might be able to help us!"

"May I advise caution?" Ms. VAIN suggested. "There are stories in which distant lights are a positive, but many more where they can mean trouble. Will-o'-the-wisps, jack-o'-lanterns, chōchin-obake, Liekkö ... And in the natural world, anglerfish are known to ..."

Cleo ignored her. She was already sprinting down the passage, waving her free hand and whooping to try to get the thing's attention. Yorick couldn't possibly keep up, so after a few hundred feet, she found herself in murky gloom, halfway between both light sources without really benefiting from either. There was something unsettling about the hidden spaces above and beneath the pipes, like tunnels within tunnels, and even when they weren't rattling with their heavy contents, there was a constant stream of slithers and trickles traveling up and down the hall. Cleo skidded to a stop.

"I ... I think it's coming this way," she whispered.

And it was.

CHAPTER SIXTEEN

leo had to shield her eyes as it got close. Its beams were stronger than Yorick's, and she couldn't get a good look at it because of the glare. A few things were for sure, though: it was big, it was fast, and it knew Cleo was there. A low-pitched thrumming, almost like a man groaning in pain, filled the passage, and it set Cleo's heart to racing. She backed up a step, and then another. At her movement, the thing surged forward, coming to a stop about twenty feet away. As its light filled the passage, she saw it clearly.

"Um . . . Ms. VAIN," Cleo whispered.

"Yes, love?"

"In—in any of your stories . . . did the sources of the good light look like this?"

She held up her scroll, hands trembling.

"No, dear," Ms. VAIN said quietly. "No, they did not."

It was a drone—that was obvious. Eight glassy, spiderlike eyes bulged from its front plate, and the arachnid similarities didn't end there. Haloed around its head were long, telescoping appendages, each ending in a different tool: a claw, a net, a shovel blade, a nozzle, a wire brush . . .

And a barbed spear tip.

As Cleo stared, the thing rotated through them all, spinning them until two settled beneath its head like arms. These two—the spear and the claw—began to flex and adjust.

Cleo stepped back farther.

The drone crept forward, training its eye beams on her, and it lifted itself higher, bringing both tools in line with Cleo's head. As it did, she was able to see beneath it. In the same space where a spider's bulbous abdomen would hang, the drone had a sack of tight netting. To Cleo's horror, that netting rippled and pulsed, moving in a way much too organic for a drone.

There was something alive in there.

Many things.

Cleo screamed. The drone loomed over her.

She ran.

Poor Yorick, who had just managed to catch up, found himself swept out of the way, and he careened into the wall, hitting it with a solid thump before falling to the concrete floor. The drone ignored him, racing after Cleo and easily cutting the distance. Cleo dared a look over her shoulder.

It was right there.

She dove to the ground just as its claw snapped at her shoulder, the concrete floor tearing at her hands and knees. Frantic, Cleo rolled to the side as it came back for another pass, and she found herself wedged beneath the lowermost pipe, her pillowcase shielding her chest. She tried to make herself as small as she could, to squirm her way as deeply into that crevice as possible. She held her breath, even though her lungs burned, and peeked out.

The drone hovered there, slowly spinning as it sought her. The thing's belly sack was clearly visible now, and Cleo could see what it contained: dozens and dozens of rats. They squeaked, fought, and crawled over one another, tearing and scrambling to find an opening that wasn't there. And something bigger: a furry thing with a black-banded tail, intelligent eyes, and long fingers that curled around the fibers of the net. A wave of pity for the captured creatures washed over Cleo, followed by fascination: these were the first animals she had ever seen outside the simulator, unless dead worms counted. But she blinked both emotions away, lest they cause her to cry out and reveal herself. It was a lost cause, though . . .

Yorick made sure of that.

"No!" Cleo hissed when she saw him. He flew erratically, as though he was dazed from his collision with the wall, but he dipped and looped his way along anyway, until he clanged into the rear of the bigger drone. It pivoted instantly, and as it did, its arms ratcheted into a new arrangement. The net arm shot forward, scooping Yorick out of the air. When the skull was entangled, the little drone inside buzzed indignantly. The bigger drone lifted the net up and over its back, and Cleo heard a hatch or hole or something open, likely so that it could dump Yorick down into its belly sack. But Yorick, it seemed, couldn't be bothered to comply. As soon as the drone tried to drop him in, he simply took off, humming his way along the back side of the spidery thing before floating to the ground.

And staring right at Cleo.

When the big drone heard the click of the skull on the floor, it spun again, lowering its lenses to the ground. Yorick, fighting to stay aloft, bumped and glided along the concrete, his beams shining directly into Cleo's face.

Soon, so too did the spider drone's.

A terrible, ear-piercing keen erupted from the thing, and its claw arm shot into Cleo's space. She kicked at it, knocking it upward against the pipe. It responded by sweeping another arm through the crack, bringing its net over Cleo's head and jerking her forward. But she was bigger than the rats and other animals it preyed on, and it couldn't drag her out, though the tugging most definitely hurt. Cleo reached up and ripped at the netting. She grabbed the metal frame of the arm and twisted, heaved, and yanked every bit as hard as the drone did. And with an abrupt shredding sound, the arm came off. The drone shuddered and pulled back.

"Go away!" Cleo screamed. "Go!"

It cycled through its arms again. Cleo thought to use the delay to scramble out, maybe to try and run.

She never got the chance.

A blast of liquid, stinging and hot, erupted from the nozzle at the end of the drone's newest arm. Cleo was forced to cover her face, bringing the pillowcase up to protect her eyes. As soon as she did, the drone's claw darted forward, grabbing the fabric of the bag and pulling. Cleo tried to fight, but the spray of liquid hurt everywhere it touched, and she didn't dare open her eyes or mouth. To her horror, the huge drone managed to rip the pillowcase away. Before she could grab it, the thing swept it up and dropped it into its sack. Cleo spat and wiped at her eyes with her sleeve, but by the time she could see, the drone had already taken off down the passage, either satisfied with its haul or in search of repairs. Cleo scurried from beneath the pipe and gave chase, but it was too fast, and when it turned a corner, she lost it.

And the pillowcase.

And everything inside it.

CHAPTER SEVENTEEN

Her hands were bleeding, and where the liquid the drone had sprayed touched a cut, it burned. Cleo twisted her shirt around so that the dry back was in front, and she wrapped up her hands in the loose fabric over her belly. Yorick skipped and skittered across the floor, settling near her as best he could. One of his lights was much dimmer than the other, and there was an awkward clicking coming from inside the skull every time he tried to fly. Still, he provided enough brightness for Cleo to see where she had dropped her scroll, and she gingerly pulled it from beneath the pipe.

"Ms. VAIN, it's all gone," Cleo said softly.

"I know. I was able to see."

"What . . . what was that thing?"

"A cleanser drone."

Cleo shivered and looked down the hallway. "Are . . . are there lots of them?"

Ms. VAIN blinked, then took a sip from the mug on her desk. "That information isn't in the database. I can bring up the design schematics if you like, though."

Cleo winced when Ms. VAIN disappeared, replaced by the menacing face of the cleanser drone. Still, she forced herself to study the diagram. And what she saw wasn't all bad news.

"That stuff it sprayed me with was just hot, soapy water," Cleo said.

"Yes. According to the description, they use it to flush nests of animals from between the pipes. Then they capture and remove them. Apparently, vermin are an issue on these lower levels."

"White blood cells . . . ," Cleo murmured.

"What of them, love?"

"Just thinking," Cleo replied. "If the transport drones are red blood cells, and the repair drones are platelets, that thing was a white blood cell."

"A monocyte, perhaps? They are the largest, and they absorb anything invasive."

Cleo nodded. "It had them—rats and something bigger—in a net. That's where it put my pillowcase." She took a deep breath, blinking back more tears. "And Silky Blanket. And the last of the medicine."

"When you think about it, that's a humane solution."

"Humane?" Cleo asked.

"Yes; the drone could easily exterminate the pests, but it doesn't."

Cleo sat up straighter. "I wonder what it does with what it catches . . ."

"There's no record of that, either. More's the pity."

"I need to think," Cleo said, and she closed her eyes. She tried to imagine where in a system of veins and arteries a white blood cell might go after absorbing a bacterium or virus, but she found it hard to visualize. Instead, a very different image popped into her mind: the engorged belly of a sleeping wolf.

And the hunter, ax in hand, standing over it.

Leaping to her feet, Cleo grabbed Yorick and cradled him under her arm. She rolled her scroll closed and tucked it into the waistband of her pants. Then she swept up the long, spindly net arm, swung it through the air like a sword, and nodded.

It was time to hunt.

CHAPTER EIGHTEEN

Cleo stalked down the corridor after the cleanser, gritting her teeth and swinging the net arm against the pipes every dozen feet or so. They rang hollowly, creating a pattern of eerie echoes that announced her presence.

"Where are you?" she growled. "I'm not supposed to be here! Come 'cleanse' me!"

Nothing came.

Despite her frustration, Cleo did notice that the pipes became more numerous. They flanked her on both sides now, and they had widened, too. They reminded her of muscle fibers, packed tight and long. She couldn't even crawl under one to hide now.

Not that she meant to hide.

Without a trail to follow, though, Cleo was left to guess at every intersection. And without Ms. VAIN recording, she knew she could be getting herself in deeper trouble with each step. But she had to get that medicine back, so she let the pipes lead her. Every few minutes, they gurgled, and the sound let her know in which direction the contents of the tubes were headed. She was surer by the second that the pipes transported waste and compost away from the units, and if that was true, she figured the cleanser drone might take its cargo to the same place. At least, that was what she hoped.

Her suspicions were confirmed by her nose. A sharp smell, like spoiled apple juice and overcooked spinach, filled the passage. Cleo was forced to cover her face with her sleeve, breathing through the fabric. It didn't help much.

"Be thankful you don't have olfactory receptors," Cleo muttered to Yorick. He knocked about a bit within the skull but didn't have the power to pull away.

Another fifty feet down the passage, Cleo was able to detect a definite increase in temperature, too. Just outside of home, she had felt comfortable, even slightly cool. Now, though, she was sweating, which only made the little cuts on her knees and palms sting all the more. A droplet trickled into her eye, and she had to put Yorick down to wipe at her brow. His light went out briefly, revealing something else farther down the passage.

The brighter lights of a cleanser drone.

"Hey!" Cleo shouted, and she grabbed Yorick by the eye sockets. With a snarl, she closed the distance on the drone; it had slowed considerably.

Almost too late, she found out why.

The hallway opened onto a huge room, lit only by the sweeping light beams of a dozen cleanser drones. Gaping pipes jutted from the walls, and every few moments one of them spewed its contents into a rectangular pit—a pit Cleo nearly tumbled into as she hurtled forward. She stopped right at the edge.

The damaged cleanser drone sailed slowly over it.

"Come back here!" Cleo demanded. The drone ignored her. Instead, it lowered itself into the pit, until it was just a few feet above a heaping mound of whatever the pipes had unloaded. Cleo dropped to her hands and knees to peek over the edge.

The piles, it turned out, were compost. Apple cores, peanut shells, kale stalks, potato skins, wilted lettuce— anything and everything not eaten by the people in Cleo's building. The smell that blasted up from the pit turned Cleo's stomach, but she forced herself to keep watching. The drone settled on a pile like a bird on its nest, and its netting fell away. A tangle of rats tumbled out, scurrying off or digging into the pile. The larger creature stood on its hind legs and chittered angrily at the drone, then grabbed a partially chewed plum and retreated. The drone lifted off, leaving only one thing at the top of the compost heap.

Cleo's pillowcase.

The drop, she decided quickly, wasn't bad—about ten feet or so. If she landed in one of the piles, she figured it wouldn't even hurt much. But that was only half the equation. Getting out again? She had no idea how she'd manage that.

And she didn't have time to figure it out, either.

Just as Cleo sat up, another cleanser spotted her. Its blinding lights swept over the edge of the pit, then locked on Cleo. It swooped at her, its brush-and-nozzle arms extended.

Cleo smashed it in the face with her net-sword.

Blue sparks replaced its light beams, and the plastic from three of its eyes shattered and tumbled off the ledge.

"Sorry!" Cleo said reflexively. "I didn't want to hurt you! Just . . . go away!"

If the thing understood, it didn't let on. Instead, it switched appendages, bringing the spear tip to bear. It jabbed at her, and she responded with a second swing. It caught the spear arm right at the joint, snapping it in two. She screamed at the drone, flailing wildly with her weapon until it, too, broke, the net stuck in the dead center of the cleanser drone's front plate.

Suddenly defenseless, Cleo jumped back into the hallway, expecting the drone to give chase. But it didn't. Instead, it hovered there, its arms limp and lights out. After a few moments, it spun about slowly, ascending and making its way toward an opening in the ceiling. It was joined in midair by two of the little repair drones, which escorted it the rest of the way out of the chamber.

"Thank you!" Cleo called after them.

Three more cleansers swiveled, their lights locking on her simultaneously. Cleo turned to run.

Another spidery drone had floated in behind her, belly net full and wriggling.

She leaped off the edge just as the lead cleanser reached her, its spear stabbing where her spine had just been. Cleo landed on her feet, but the compost was so soft beneath her that she couldn't keep her balance. Her hands sank into the mess up to her elbows, and Yorick rolled away. Cleo spun onto her back, kicking and punching upward.

The drones ignored her.

As she panted, the cleanser from the hallway sailed overhead. When it reached the far side of the pit, it descended. Like the one Cleo had fought in the tunnel, it deposited its net of creatures, then left. Even though a dozen rats scattered over the compost, none of the cleansers paid them any attention. The pit, she realized, was safe.

Or safe from the cleanser drones, at least.

Cleo slogged her way to the pillowcase, grabbing Yorick along the way. She had to swat at a mean-looking rat before she picked the skull up, and it nipped at her, barely missing her hand. Two more rats had started exploring her pillowcase, and she pushed them away with her foot.

"You're surrounded by food!" Cleo snapped. "Go find some other nastiness to nibble."

With the pillowcase retrieved, she did her best to clean off her fingers, wiping the warm, wet compost juice on her pants. Then, whispering a little prayer, she yanked her bag open and peered inside. Her silky blanket was wadded up tightly, and nestled in the middle, still unbroken, was the final medicine sphere. Cleo whooped with relief, then growled at another rat that had snuck up to see what the commotion was. As it fell over itself to get away, Cleo had to laugh.

She was lost, terrified, bruised, and stuck at the bottom of a compost pit, but she felt triumphant. Wrapping her fingers around the softness of the pillowcase, she closed her eyes and allowed herself to enjoy this small victory.

Her respite lasted only a moment.

A grinding screech echoed through the chamber, so loud it forced Cleo to cover her ears. And then, it seemed, the entire world turned upside down. The floor tilted suddenly, transforming the compost into an avalanche of sticky rot, and Cleo was rolled along with it, buried under the tumbling, festering pile. She clung to the pillowcase and Yorick, spitting and writhing as she felt the compost cover her face and trap her limbs. With a heave of revulsion, she twisted—there was something scratching and scrambling at her back, though it was borne away as the mound flowed over itself, funneling down into wherever the floor was designed to dump them.

CHAPTER NINETEEN

The heat was unbearable.

There was no air to breathe.

And she couldn't move.

She had landed somewhere soft—that much she knew. She had even bounced a few times before a cascade of compost poured over her, blotting out the light and everything else. Now she was completely covered, and worse, she could feel the blanket of debris getting heavier by the moment. So she squirmed, ratlike, pumping with her legs and raking with her arms until she cleared a little space. And what room she cleared, she claimed—digging, almost swimming through the stinking pile. Wet things, slimy things pressed in, wriggling against her cheeks, sliding through her fingers, and threatening to invade her mouth every time her lips parted.

But still, she fought.

And with one last explosion of effort, she burst free.

Her eyes opened just long enough for her to see the drop beneath her—she was on the side of a steep hill of compost, one that started green but browned as it went down.

As *she* went down.

She rolled most of the way, only once even attempting to slow herself, which just resulted in Cleo flipping head over heels. Realizing that was useless, she wrapped herself around the pillowcase and gave in to gravity. It took her all the way to solid ground, and a dozen feet past the end of the pile. She came to rest in something soft, something that surrounded her without covering her. Something that felt familiar.

She reached out with a grime-covered hand, casting about without daring to lift her head or open her eyes.

"G-grass?" Cleo mumbled. She allowed her fingers to curl around the slender, cool blades of it, and she twisted gently. There was a soft ripping noise, like buttons popping off a shirt, and a thatch of the stuff came away in her fist. Only then did she sit up and look.

It was as if she had woken up in the simulator—only somehow, *more*.

A tuft of vibrant green rustled in her hand, and she spread her fingers, letting it flutter to the ground. Several blades were caught by a breeze and flew away to settle near a patch of puffy-headed yellow flowers. Cleo had to squint to see it all—it was so bright! And that breeze . . . it was strange, uneven, almost swirling, not at all like the regulated puffs of air that the simulator emitted. It seemed to play with Cleo's hair joyfully, knocking a few old spinach leaves out of her tangle. She shivered with the sensation of it.

And then she looked up.

In all her twelve years, Cleo had never seen anything so vast. So undefinable. It was blue in a way that nothing else could possibly be—not the medicine, not her father's eyes, and certainly not the sky in the simulator. This . . . this *everywhere* . . . it seemed to mock the work of her father and all the other artists who had tried to capture it. It was impossibly wide, infinitely high, and completely full . . . full of color, and sound, and difference.

A wave of dizziness struck Cleo as she tried to take it all in. She didn't know where to tell her eyes to focus, because each thing she saw had something new just behind it. Everything she heard was followed instantly by a stranger sound farther off, or to the side, or behind her. It all started to blend together, and to spin.

Cleo closed her eyes.

She leaned over.

And she got sick on the grass.

She let it come, allowing her body to cope in whatever way it decided was best. And when she was done, when she was empty, she found that she felt better. The breeze on her skin was soothing, and the sun above her—the real, honest-to-goodness *sun*—warmed her, which helped with her shivering. Then she dared to open her eyes again.

Everything was less spinny the second time around, and Cleo exhaled slowly, concentrating on getting her breathing right so that she didn't hyperventilate again. She used her own body as a point of reference, staring at her hands first. They were profoundly dirty. Blood from the cuts had mixed with compost and grass and dirt, and she could feel it thick under her fingernails and sticky in the creases of her palms.

Infection, her mind warned her. *Influenza D.*

Cleo lifted the neck of her shirt up, covering her mouth and nose, and squinted at the air around her, as if she expected to see a massive bacteria cloud descending on her. Then she reached slowly for her pillowcase.

The tin that contained the first aid kit was dented, but the contents—gauze, topical ointments, and a thermometer patch—seemed okay. She poured some of her remaining water into her palms and wrung them together, wincing as her scrapes were opened anew. More blood welled in the wounds, but she knew that was good; it flushed out the bacteria and anything else that didn't belong there. Taking a steadying breath, she uncapped a tube of the strongest antiseptic in the tin and squirted it into her hands.

Then she rubbed.

The pain was so sharp her eyes watered, and she thought she might be sick again. But her body held, and she managed to get some of the gauze wrapped around the worst spots. She repeated the process for her knees. Her falls had ripped the fabric away so badly that she could get to her skin without even having to hitch up her pant legs.

"I'm a mess," she muttered. Her voice sounded strange to her, words lost in all the openness, and the lack of any reply sent a pang of loneliness through her. Instinctively, she reached for her scroll.

It wasn't there.

"Ms. VAIN?" Cleo cried, and she scanned the grass around her. Nothing. She checked her pillowcase, but she knew that was a lost cause; she clearly remembered shoving her scroll in the waistband of her pants. That meant if it wasn't here, it was in the compost heap.

Or, Cleo thought as she looked up, the compost *mountain*.

But still, despite its height, it wasn't even close to the most striking thing she saw. That was the massive black cube behind it. It startled her so badly she tumbled backward, scooting away a few feet as she craned her neck. How could she not have noticed it before? But it rose into a different part of the sky (*There's even* more *sky*, Cleo marveled), and the lowest parts were hidden by the compost. Its sheer size made Cleo forget for a moment about Ms. VAIN, about Yorick and Miriam Wendemore-Adisa and her own plight.

It was the biggest thing she'd ever seen.

And, she realized, it was her home.

Every inch of the building, which extended as far as she could see in either direction, was covered in shiny blackness. It was mirrorlike, so that Cleo saw in its surface the same sky, the same clouds, the same grass and compost as she did when she snuck a glance behind her. It reached so high that she had to shield her eyes against the sun to see the top, and she noticed it went higher still, as huge towers sprouted from its roof, each one capped by a wheel of spinning blades. *Windmills,* Cleo thought. *Like in the village in our game.*

Lower down, Cleo spotted the opening that belched forth the compost. It was about twenty feet up, and every so often another reeking pile of the stuff was disgorged from the opening onto the mound, where it ran down the sides of the cone. Cleo watched it intently, trying to figure out where Ms. VAIN might have ended up, or Yorick.

Midway up the mountain, she spotted a grinning, skeletal face.

"Yorick!" she shouted, and she leaped to her feet. They were unsteady, and she wobbled for a moment, but she gritted her teeth and forced herself to concentrate on that skull. Launching herself up the pile, she scrambled and clawed her way through the mess until her fingertips thrust through the open jaw. She yanked him out, then slid her way back down to the ground. Her hands shaking, she dared to look inside.

The little drone spun around, buzzed at her, and settled. Yorick was safe.

Ms. VAIN, however, was nowhere to be found. Cleo spent another five minutes pacing back and forth along the pile, looking up whenever her vision stopped spinning. She found it helped to walk, and to have an immediate purpose. In fact, Cleo could barely feel the effects of her surroundings by the time she sat down again.

But that was only because she was so nervous about Ms. VAIN that it pushed all the other worries to the side.

"Do you see her, Yorick?" she asked the drone, holding him up and toward the pile. His rotors whirred to life, and when she let go, he hovered there, but he didn't make a beeline toward any place in particular. He was probably so confused that he was paralyzed, Cleo thought. After all, everything out here was an anomaly . . .

"Maybe . . . maybe she fell down the other side?" Cleo muttered, and she picked up her pillowcase. Yorick continued to float there, dumbfounded, so she snagged him out of the air and tucked him under her arm. Then she set out to circumnavigate the mountain of refuse.

A hiss in the grass to her left stopped her almost immediately. Cleo froze, holding Yorick up as though she meant to throw him. From out of the knee-high grass stalked a creature, not much bigger than the ring-tailed one caught in the cleanser drone's net. This one's tail was longer, though, and it swept the air as if it had a mind of its own.

"A cat?" Cleo wondered. It certainly looked like one of the options in Tessa's pet sim game, though this one was far more scraggly. It looked at Cleo balefully, hissed again, and then leaped past her. She jumped out of the way in time to see it pounce on a hapless rat, one that had just rolled down the compost. The rat didn't even have a chance to get back on its feet before the cat was dragging it into the grass. Cleo shuddered.

As she walked, she spotted at least a dozen more cats. They slouched at the edge of the grass line, bodies low and tails raised. Whenever a fresh deluge of compost tumbled out the opening, their backsides would wiggle back and forth, and then they'd shoot out at the pile, fighting and yowling over which ones got the fattest mice or the slowest rats.

"Maybe not quite so humane . . . ," Cleo said. "Though I suppose cats have to eat too, Yorick."

Despite everything, her stomach decided to rumble just then as well. But the thought of food, especially so close to a gigantic pile of rot, made her queasy all over again, so she tried to quiet her body with a sip of water. She knew it wouldn't work for long, but it was better than nothing, and it gave her the willpower to keep skirting the edge of the pile.

Unfortunately, the other side looked identical to the first—cats, rats, and all. There was no sign of Ms. VAIN.

And, Cleo noted, the sun wasn't as bright as it had been just a little while ago. Instinctively, she thought to ask Ms. VAIN the time, and the sheer weight of her teacher's absence felt like a punch to the chest. She set Yorick down next to her pillowcase and began frantically burrowing into the compost, ripping away layers of stinking decay. But the hole she dug yielded nothing but heat, more stench, and handfuls of fat, wriggling worms, the sight of which made her feel all the worse.

She had been silly back then, when she had tried to save one.

What did that make her now?

Eventually, she slumped against the black wall of the building itself, tired and sore and afraid. The light really was dwindling, and Yorick's beams clicked on automatically. Cleo pulled him into her lap and hung her head. This time, there was no teacher to comfort her. Only the rats and cats and the whole entire immeasurable world around her.

Which, apparently, was full of bugs.

Cleo hadn't noticed them before, probably because she was so overwhelmed by everything else. But as the sun dropped, clouds of them formed, swarming around the compost and around her. Most of them moved too quickly for her to see as anything other than traces in the air, but some of them settled on her arms and legs. She peered at one that had landed on her wrist. It twitched around the tiny hairs on her arm as though it was getting comfortable.

Then it bit her.

"Hey!" Cleo cried, and she brushed it off. It flew a little way and tried to land on her ankle. When she looked, she saw three more of them already there. She flicked her hand at these as well, and as she moved, she noticed a sudden, powerful itch on her wrist. The spot where the first one had stuck its needlelike nose had swelled.

mosquitos
ñ ñ

"Dermal pruritus and edema?" she said. As if on cue, her ankle started burning as well. She raked her finger-nails along the bumps, but that only relieved the itchiness temporarily . . .

. . . and revealed two more of the bugs on her hands.

"Agh!" Cleo yelled, and she leaped up, shaking her arms and legs wildly. A swarm of the insects poofed away from her, emitting a whiny hum ten times more aggravating than anything Yorick ever managed. Then they descended on her again. She thought about running, but the idea of leaving her building terrified her.

So she crammed her hand into her pillowcase, pulled out her silky blanket, and threw it over her head.

As she checked the sphere of medicine and used her first aid kit to reapply disinfectant to her cuts, carefully removing and then replacing the gauze, Cleo could hear the bugs flying around outside her makeshift tent. It seemed they couldn't penetrate the blanket, though. She sighed with relief and tucked the extra fabric beneath her feet and bottom, trapping the rest against the wall of the building with her back.

Then she waited.

And she squirmed.

And she scratched.

All told, she counted fourteen bites. Most were on her arms, but the ones by her ankles itched more. There was one on her neck, too, in a spot her hair didn't cover. She knew scratching wasn't a good idea, but she couldn't help it, especially since it helped distract her from the other night-time noises.

Just beyond the veil of her blanket, it sounded like a nightmare. The compost chute screeched deafeningly every half hour or so, and that set off a chain reaction of squeaking rats, yowling cats, and storms of buzzing insects so loud that Cleo thought she could feel her brain vibrating. Each time, she tried to shrink herself smaller, to press tighter to the black shell that covered her home.

It was a new sound that scared her out from under the blanket—a gravelly crunching that banished all the other noises. She jumped to her feet and pointed Yorick toward the end of the compost pile. Nothing was visible yet, but that sound got closer and closer. Finally, when it seemed as though she'd have to drop Yorick and cover her ears, the source of the noise burst into view.

It was a drone—or at least as near as Cleo could tell. Unlike Yorick or any of the others she had seen inside, though, this one didn't fly. Instead, it rolled forward on massive black tires. They spun in two tracks of dry ground, and as it approached, little stones and clumps of grass shot to either side. Cleo had to lift her blanket to guard her face, and she skittered back a dozen feet along the wall, giving the thing plenty of room.

When the drone reached the pile, its front plate split in two, like the yawning jaws of some huge beast—a dragon, maybe, or one of those huge, fat river animals from a fable

Ms. VAIN once told ... hippos, she thought they were called. It lowered that heavy jaw to the ground and then rammed into the compost, swallowing up a greedy mouthful. Cleo could hear its gears grinding as it drew the rotting food in, and then it pulled away, front plate sealing closed once more. Lumbering backward, it kicked up another cloud of grass and dust and disappeared.

Cleo thought to chase it down—what if it had eaten Ms. VAIN? But she was too frightened. Too tired.

And the bugs had found her again.

Miserable, Cleo hid under her blanket once more. She did her best to nibble on her last apple, but it was so bruised, and the flesh so mealy, that she could barely get it down. There wasn't anything to help with itching in her first aid kit, either, so she was left to sit and suffer. It did help to remind herself that Ms. VAIN wasn't truly lost—her scroll was. Ms. VAIN existed in the network. Right now, she was probably answering a hundred million questions from ten thousand kids, who took her soft lavender sweater and kindly eyes for granted.

In fact, it was while imagining Ms. VAIN, sitting at her desk and leafing through a thick book to find a story, that Cleo finally fell asleep, curled into a sorry little ball at the foot of a home she couldn't reach.

CHAPTER TWENTY

She felt something on her shoulder—a rhythmic tapping.

Light.

Gentle.

At least, at first.

Cleo blinked awake, her eyes focusing on the sliver of light that snuck beneath her blanket. The next jab sent a jolt of pain up her arm, and Cleo threw away her blanket, sitting up and grabbing at the stick that waved in her face.

"Sweet mercy, you're alive!" someone exclaimed.

Cleo screamed in reply.

The person in front of her screamed, too, and whacked Cleo on the head with the stick. It wasn't a particularly strong blow, but it hurt, and it sent Cleo scrambling back along the wall, her hands up and teeth bared.

As her eyes adjusted to the fierce brightness of daylight,

Cleo saw who had struck her. It was a woman, no taller than Cleo but vastly older. She held the stick up like a spear, its tip waving unsteadily before her deeply wrinkled face.

Cleo couldn't help but stare. Other than her mom and dad, this was the first person she had ever actually laid eyes on.

"Are . . . are you real?" Cleo murmured after a moment.

"What?" the woman snapped.

Cleo repeated the question.

"Come any closer and I'll show you!" the woman said, her gnarled hands twisting around the base of her stick. "Are *you* real?"

Cleo nodded.

"Happened again, has it?"

? what happened again . . .

"Wha—"

The woman hocked and spat on the ground, then cast her head about slowly. "Knew it would. Where're the rest of you? Already run off?"

"The . . . the rest of me? Run off?" Cleo asked raggedly. "I don't know what any of that means!"

Thrusting the tip of her stick into the ground, the woman hobbled forward. Cleo retreated, but she soon found herself trapped between the black wall of the structure and the reeking mound of compost to her left.

"What went wrong?" the woman pressed. "Power go out? Sickness get in?"

"Sickness?" Cleo echoed, and her eyes went wide. She clawed at the front of her shirt, bringing it over her face again. Peeking out above the neckline, she held her other hand up to ward the woman away. "Are . . . are you infected?"

"My question first," the woman countered. "Where are your people?"

Before Cleo could respond, the compost chute gave a great, pneumatic *whoosh* and spewed another load of rats and rot on top of the pile. Some of it rolled down toward Cleo, forcing her to dance out of the way before it buried her anew. When she turned back, the woman hadn't moved.

"Well, kid?"

Cleo moved her shirt away from her mouth just long enough to point. "In there."

The woman grumbled, reaching up to run her bent fingers through a thatch of gray hair. Then, with great effort, she hunkered down and sat in the grass. She rested her stick across her lap as she crossed her legs. Huddled like that, it was hard for Cleo to tell where her body stopped and her neck began. She seemed bunched together, a severely rounded back, wide shoulders, and a pot belly all draped by a purple-and-green dress. Her shoes were strange, too—colorful, with thick rubber soles and sides that reached past the woman's splotchy, skinny ankles. There were laces, but they were untied.

"Got a name, kid?" the woman asked.

"In-influenza D . . ."

"Sweet mercy . . . that's the worst name I've ever heard! Whose parents name them after an epidemic? What's your middle name, tuberculosis?"

"No," Cleo replied. "You might have influenza D."

The woman sneered. "Please. Nobody's had that for fifty years. Now pull that shirt off your face and tell me your name."

Cleo stared at her for a few moments. Perhaps she was right. It seemed hard to believe that anyone could have influenza D and live to be as old as her, much less have enough strength to bop Cleo on the head. Grudgingly, Cleo let the shirt fall from her mouth.

"I'm Cleo."

"Well, Cleo, I don't see a gaping hole in your building, or a terrible fire, or a bunch of corpses sliding out of that chute," the woman said, and she used her stick to point at the towering building. "But something must have gone wrong."

Cleo grabbed her pillowcase from the ground and held it tight to her chest for comfort. "Why do you keep saying that? Nothing went wrong!"

"And yet you're here. How'd that happen, eh?"

"I . . . ," Cleo murmured, running her filthy fingertips along the shape of Yorick inside the pillowcase. "I made mistakes."

The woman was seized by a coughing fit, or so Cleo thought. But then she realized the hoarse, wheezing jags were actually laughter.

"Mistakes? I should say so!"

Cleo glanced up at the chute. "I need to get back inside."

That brought another round of hacking laughter.

"Please help me," Cleo blurted. The old woman's snickers died away. At the very end, she sniffled and spat again into the grass.

"You're really here by accident, aren't you?"

Cleo nodded pathetically.

"And alone?"

"I have ...," Cleo started. She squeezed at the lump in her pillowcase. "Yes. I'm alone."

The woman squinted at her.

Cleo blushed and opened her bag. "I guess ... I guess you could count Yorick. He's an observation drone. I keep him inside this skull so—"

"Sweet mercy!"

Cleo flinched. The woman had raised her stick again, and she was pointing it right at Yorick. "Where did you get that, girl? And why on earth are you lugging it around? You're ... you're not *imbalanced,* are you?"

"It's a model," Cleo explained.

"For heaven's sake, get a doll or a blanket like a normal child!"

"I have a blanket ...," Cleo muttered, and she picked it up, wrapping it about herself. Something told her not to cry in front of this woman, but she found the tears coming anyway.

The woman clicked her tongue. "Yeah ... I suppose I can see that," she said. "And I'm ... well, I'm sorry. Didn't mean to hurt your feelings. You're probably upset enough ... I know I'd be clear out of my gourd if I had to live in there."

Cleo followed the path of her stick to where she pointed, right up the compost chute.

"You mean, you're *not* from inside?" Cleo whispered.

"Huh?"

"From inside," Cleo repeated louder.

"Heck no!"

"But . . ."

"But what?" she said, and she rolled her shoulders back until the joints cracked. "The flu? Lost just about everyone when it happened, of course. But there was no way they were packing me in there like a sardine. I refused. And let me tell you, not a single soul shed a tear for Angie Purnell when those solar panels sealed closed. Too busy covering their own behinds to worry about the rest of us."

Cleo looked around. "The rest of you?"

"Gone now, mostly. A few of us codgers still shuffle around out here. Most stayed shacked up in the city, but not me. Couldn't stand the stairs and the sidewalks. Bad on my knees, though I do make the trip to do a bit of trading every now and again. Like my shoes? Got 'em for two strings of bluegill. Who cares if they're eighty years old? I'm a hundred and two. Figure that lets me wear just about anything I want."

Angie wiggled her feet. Cleo gaped.

"You're a hundred and two?"

"Don't act so shocked. I got my shots and medicines just like everyone else fixing to go in. I just didn't take that last step. How old do folks on the inside get to be?"

Cleo took a deep breath and set her jaw. "I'm . . . I'm not *that* shocked. According to the database, average life expectancy for a woman is one hundred nineteen years."

"Hooray for me, then."

"And you've been out here all this time, alone?"

Angie nodded and slapped at a fly. "More or less."

"More or less?"

"That's right, and that's all I'm fixing to tell a creepy skull kid at the moment."

Sheepishly, Cleo slipped Yorick back into her pillowcase. He buzzed a bit, but quieted soon after. Clearing her throat, Cleo said, "Are you going to help me or not?"

Angie rested her stick across her lap and crossed her arms.

"Turn around, Cleo. You see a door?"

She didn't have to look to know the answer. She gritted her teeth, wiped at her eyes, and shook her head.

"Exactly. Place was built to keep people out."

Cleo's tears began to fall, picking up the grime from her cheeks and leaving little trails. A wave of dizziness struck her, and she let her suddenly wobbly legs guide her to the ground. She curled her arms around her pillowcase and pressed her face to her knees.

Angie's face puckered, a thousand wrinkles joining the countless others around her eyes. With a profound groan, she pulled herself to her feet and shuffled forward. Her hand trembled softly as she reached down to pat Cleo's shoulder.

"You seem like a smart kid. Driven, certainly, to get all the way out here."

Cleo shivered.

"Yeah," Angie said, heaving a sigh. "I think I can help you."

Cleo looked up, the moisture in her eyes blurring Angie's figure. "You can?"

Angie coughed and looked away. She took a deep breath, one that seemed to expand her entire body, and then she tapped the ground with her stick twice. Gruffly, she said, "Probably gonna come back to bite me in the behind, but yeah." She turned her head, staring for several moments at a spot in the tall grass, a little path where the greenery was tamped down. As Cleo watched, Angie mumbled something, then snapped her gaze back to Cleo and nodded. "First, though, you have to help me. I've lost nearly my entire morning, and the fish don't bite once the sun is high."

"Help you how?"

Angie stabbed her stick at the compost pile. "Worms. Need 'em for bait."

Cleo stood slowly. Angie ambled to the edge of the grass, where she had stashed a rusty metal bucket. The old woman hissed as she wrapped her crooked fingers around the handle, and it took her a long time to get a proper grip. When she finally had it, she padded back to Cleo and held the bucket out. Cleo stared at her hand. The joints were swollen, and each finger seemed to zigzag away from the others, rather than line up in a neat row around the wooden handle.

"Here. Take it," Angie insisted, and Cleo fumbled with it before pulling it in. It was empty.

"Gotta get at least a hundred night crawlers in there. I don't want to have to come back tomorrow. Too long a walk."

Cleo stared at her.

"Well . . . get to digging!"

Angie brushed past her and shoved her stick into the compost pile, swirling it around until the top layer of detritus was cleared. Just beneath was a rich, loamy brown, where decomposition had transformed the leftover food into a cakey soil. It took only a few moments for the worms to appear, their pink, bulbous heads poking out into the air.

"Grab 'em, Cleo! My hands won't do," Angie barked.

Cleo jumped in, snagging one of the wriggling heads and tugging. To her amazement, the worm just kept coming; it was much bigger than those she had seen yesterday or the one in her father's grass box. As she held it up, watching it lash back and forth, she found she was able to see its internal organs.

"I think those are its aortic arches . . ." Cleo pointed.

"Don't care. Into the bucket with him," Angie replied. Cleo dropped the worm in, wincing as it plunked at the bottom.

So many were the worms that it took Cleo only a few minutes to collect the other ninety-nine Angie demanded— plus one "for good luck." Grinning—and showing off her remaining eight teeth—Angie patted Cleo on the shoulder.

"Good work. Now let's go."

"To the door?"

Angie sighed. "Told you, girl. There is no door."

Cleo frowned. "But you said—"

"That I'd help you. And I will. But I've got a hundred hooks to set before noon. If I don't, then I'm behind. Nothing to catch. Nothing to trade. And less to eat."

Angie started off, chattering all the way. She didn't realize Cleo wasn't with her until she was waist-high in the grass. "Child, are you coming or not?" she yelled over her shoulder.

Cleo slapped a hand against the black wall behind her. "Not!"

Angie scowled, then looked skyward. "You only send me the thickheaded ones, is that right?" she murmured.

"I have to get back in there!"

The old woman shambled up to Cleo, who dropped the bucket with a noisy clang. It almost tipped, but Angie thrust her stick down to settle it. The worms knotted and twisted together until there was no telling where one ended and another began.

"Why?" Angie grumbled. "What's so important—"

"This," Cleo replied sharply, and she picked up her pillowcase. From inside she pulled the remaining sphere of calotexina florinase. "It's the whole reason I'm out here. Whole reason I left home in the first place."

"To play ball?"

"No!" Cleo shouted. Angie didn't react. "I mean, it's

not a ball. It's medicine. For someone named Miriam Wendemore-Adisa. I'm afraid she'll die without it."

"Who is she to you? Your sister? Mother? Grandma?"

Cleo shrugged. "I don't know her."

Angie chuckled. "Yep. Thickheaded. Why sacrifice your safety, your home . . . heck, your entire life . . . for this lady?"

Cleo squared her shoulders and took a deep breath. "She's my patient."

As she recounted her story, from the moment the medicine arrived to waking up with Angie's stick prodding her shoulder, Angie listened patiently. If she was worried about her worms, she didn't let on. And when Cleo was done, Angie stared at her.

"So . . . so that's why," Cleo muttered, and she slipped the calotexina back in her bag.

"Hmm," Angie said. She stooped to pick up the bucket, and she leaned on her walking stick. "How do you know that lady isn't already dead?"

Cleo felt a lump in her throat. "I . . . I don't."

"Then you could've gone through all that for nothing."

Cleo shook her head. "It's *not* nothing," she shouted. "What if it was you that was sick? Wouldn't you want someone to help?"

Angie waved a hand in the air. "*Tsk*, girl. Fine. No need to lay on the guilt. And I know what you need."

"You do?"

Angie nodded. "You need to stop and think. To rest. Get some perspective."

Cleo clutched the pillowcase. "What? No! I don't have time . . ."

"You're panicking. And look where that's got you. Spend half your life studying for a test. Then some medicine shows up, you can't quiet your brain about it, right? So you launch yourself out into the world. Jump on a drone. Run down a passage. Fight a cleanser. Throw yourself into a compost pile. From the moment you started, you've been scrambling."

"But—"

"But nothing. You're a smart girl. Stop scrambling and *think*."

"I can't! The medicine expires tomorrow!"

"Eh, they just stick those dates on there to scare you, force you to buy more than you need. I was eating cans of beans five years after they 'expired,' and I'm still here, aren't I?"

Cleo's brow furrowed.

"Perspective, kid. You need some. I know where you can get some. Let's get these worms on the hooks and have a cup of tea. Then you can use that big brain to figure this out."

Cleo shook her head violently.

"Look, Cleo," Angie said. "I know it's hard. You've lived more life in the past three days than most people do in eighty years. Whatever else happens, you have to know you can't keep going like this. So come. Rest."

"But Miriam—"

"Is your patient. Yeah. But she's not the one you need to take care of first."

Angie reached up, her knotted hands guiding Cleo to turn around. There, in the liquid-black surface of the solar panels, she saw her reflection. Angie pointed at it with the tip of her walking stick.

"*She* is."

CHAPTER TWENTY-ONE

Angie led the way, the bucket swinging at her side and her knees cracking with every step. And even though the woman was slow, Cleo had trouble keeping up. She was dizzy, and she couldn't help but stop every few steps, peering over her shoulder to see if the structure was still there.

"Is . . . is it much farther?" Cleo asked as the path widened. The grass had given way to a proper trail, one that was littered with chunks of crumbly black stones displaced by the cresting joints of tree roots.

Angie swung around. "How much longer you think old Angie can walk? No. We're close. About a quarter mile down this road, we'll hit the driveway. Not that anybody's driving on it."

Cleo squinted. She couldn't see anything but more green ahead. And her home? It appeared no bigger than her fist behind her.

"I've . . . I've never been so far . . ."

"From home?" Angie guessed.

"From anywhere," Cleo replied softly.

Angie smirked. "Welcome to the world, Cleo."

Cleo huffed and lifted her chin, taking a few steps forward. Her heart fluttered, however, and she couldn't help but look back again.

Her building was still there, though it seemed like the earth was swallowing it, bit by bit.

"I . . . I need to rest," she admitted, leaning against a sturdy tree. Flakes of its greenish-gray bark tumbled to the ground at Cleo's feet, revealing the white of the trunk beneath. She closed her eyes for a moment and pressed her forehead to the wood, taking comfort in its texture. Her fingertips slid along the grooves and chips in the bark, and she imagined it as a wall—a solid thing, continuous and regular, unmoving and unchanging and predictable. But then a breeze whirled its way down the path, setting the trees to dancing, and the trunk groaned.

Gasping, Cleo stepped back. Her eyes flew open, and she looked up. Thousands of broad green leaves played against one another, and they mingled with those of the tree next to hers, and the next, and the next, in a wave of unending movement that extended as far as Cleo could see. How many leaves were there? And how many trees? Millions? Billions? All connected and kinetic and alive . . .

. . . *like people used to be,* Cleo thought suddenly, and she swooned.

Angie poked at her shoulder with a knobby finger. "You fixin' to pass out, kid?"

Cleo closed her eyes again, shaking off the rush of vertigo. She tried to summon the words to explain to Angie how she felt, but all she could manage was, "It's . . . it's just so *big* . . ."

Angie's mouth twisted to the side, and she shot a glance down the path.

"Yeah, well, take a deep breath, because it's about to get even bigger. C'mon."

Cleo brought her pillowcase to her chest and hugged it close. "Bigger?" she whispered.

But Angie didn't hear her. She was already weaving down the road, kicking little clumps of black stones out of the way with her rainbow shoes. Only when they reached a sharp split in the road did Angie stop. The main path kept going, but a smaller side trail ambled down a hill to their right. At the head of that trail was a box on a post. It was mostly rust, and it hung there by a single screw. Angie tapped it with her stick, offering Cleo a wink.

"Mail's a little late today," she quipped.

Cleo shook her head, confused.

Angie sighed. "Never mind. House is this way," she said, and she pointed a crooked finger down the side path. Cleo took a step in that direction, but Angie grabbed the tail of her shirt.

"Not so fast, kid," she warned, pulling Cleo back onto the road. "I'm going first. I need you to come behind me.

Count to sixty or something. Then, when you do, stop at that gate down there. You see it?"

Cleo glanced along the path. "Is that it?" she asked.

Angie nodded. "Yeah. S'pose it's not really a gate anymore. Just a fence with a big hole in it. Still, I need you to stop there, then wait for my signal to come the rest of the way."

Cleo swallowed nervously. "Why?"

"Remember when you asked me if I lived alone?"

Cleo nodded. "You said, 'More or less.'"

Angie's breath whistled through the gaps in her teeth. "Well, you're about to meet the 'less,'" she said, and left Cleo by the mailbox.

"Wait! There's . . . there's someone else?" Cleo asked.

"Sixty seconds," Angie replied without turning back.

Cleo set her pillowcase down and pressed her hands to her cheeks. Her fingertips were cold, and she could feel them shaking. "Someone else. Someone else . . . Okay . . . okay . . . there's someone else . . . ," she whispered. Another of the big green-gray trees stood just behind the mailbox, and Cleo slipped over to it. Near her foot was a long, furled-up piece of bark that had peeled away from the trunk. It reminded Cleo of her scroll. She picked it up and squeezed it. It crumbled apart satisfyingly in her hand, turning into crisp pieces that drifted down atop her filthy slippers.

"Someone else . . . ," she murmured once more.

Then she started counting.

When she hit sixty, she could no longer see Angie on the path. Cleo scooped up her pillowcase, checked the contents, and then willed her feet forward. The fence was only about as far as one of the red-to-violet hallways in her home, but it took her another minute to get there, her eyes darting and ears picking up every little sound . . .

Including a voice that wasn't Angie's.

Cleo couldn't help but dash the final few feet to the big gatepost, and she pressed herself behind it tightly, hoping it would be enough to hide her. She even reached up to gather the bloom of her hair in her hand so that it wouldn't stick out to either side and give her away. Then she closed her eyes and tried to quiet her breathing as best she could.

She heard that voice again, calling out. A strange voice. A high-pitched voice.

A child's voice.

Cleo's curiosity overcame her caution, and she twisted to peek past the gatepost. The path wound a little farther down the hill into a shallow valley. On the left, settled in the grass like old stones, were three cars. Cleo recognized them from several videos she had seen, only in those they had been gleaming, all chrome and glass and lights. These were nothing but rust and shards and caved roofs. The house was farther still, up the other side of the valley. Cleo couldn't see the lake Angie had alluded to, but she wasn't really looking for it.

No, her eyes were locked on Angie, who stood at the base of a set of simple, low stairs hewn into the side of the hill. She had put the bucket down and was gesturing with her stick, waving it in the air like she was painting a picture, or telling a story. Cleo craned to see who she might be speaking to.

After a few more gestures, Angie swept to the side, the tip of her stick pointing straight at the gatepost. "Cleo!" Angie called. "This is Paige! I'll bring her up to meet you!"

The child had been behind Angie, blocked from Cleo's view by the old woman's body. She was little, smaller still than even Angie, and certainly younger than Cleo. Her head was shaven, and the clothes she wore were a hodge-podge of yellow and green fabrics, sort of like Angie's shoes. In her arms the child held something tightly, gripping it much as Cleo did her pillowcase.

As Cleo gawked, Angie put a hand on the child's shoulder and guided her up the path.

Or, at least, she tried.

Paige stiffened after two steps, and she shook free of Angie's grip. Angie reached out, but the girl batted her away, dropping the object she held. Then she bolted, sprinting back toward the house. Mystified, Cleo watched as the child leaped up the steps two at a time. She scrambled onto the porch and disappeared inside, the door slamming loudly enough to startle a flock of birds in a nearby bush, scattering them into the sky.

Angie sighed so profoundly that Cleo could see her shoulders slump all the way from her hiding place, and she beckoned Cleo down.

"That went about as well as I expected," Angie snorted when Cleo reached her.

"That was a little girl!" Cleo exclaimed.

"Yep. I'm a regular Miss Hannigan these days," Angie grumbled.

"Who is she?"

"Miss Hannigan?"

Cleo's face scrunched. "No. The girl. Paige?"

"I said I'd help you find some perspective, didn't I?"

Cleo nodded.

"Well, that bitty child? She's your perspective."

"Huh?" Cleo muttered, her eyes still locked on the porch, searching for any sign of movement.

"Changes things, doesn't it? Meeting a kid like you."

"Like . . . like me?"

"Yeah."

Cleo bent down, scooping up the scruffy thing Paige had dropped. It was a stuffed dog, so tattered and worn that Cleo was worried it might fall apart in her hands. Instinctively, she cradled it to her chest.

There was another kid.

Outside.

Like her.

CHAPTER TWENTY-TWO

Angie kept her home as tidy as she could, but it still showed its age. The paint was peeling badly, a garden had long been given over to the weeds, and a broken porch swing hung by a lonely chain, scraping in a lazy circle on the deck whenever the breeze caught it. The lake, it turned out, was well behind the house, and Cleo was so distracted that it took Angie several pokes with her stick and a dozen "Never you minds" to navigate her down the path to the dock at the water's edge. Once there, Angie started fussing over her fishing poles while Cleo tried to keep thousands of questions from spilling out all at once.

"How old is she?"

"Dunno. Seven? Eight? Been with me going on five years now, and she was out of diapers when I found her, thank goodness."

"Found her?"

Angie dropped a line into the water and rubbed her worm-greasy hands across her shirt.

"Yeah. Found her. Kind of like you."

Cleo's eyes went wide, and she couldn't contain herself any longer. "Is . . . is she from inside? Does she remember how she got out? Can she get back in? Is that how she's going to help me?"

"Hush," Angie commanded, rapping her stick on the dock to startle Cleo into silence. Cleo clamped her own grubby hand over her mouth, but that didn't stop her from anxiously shifting from foot to foot. It set the little dock to swaying, which brought another steely stare from Angie. After a few more baited hooks, the old woman turned to Cleo.

"I don't know that Paige is going to be much help to you, girl. Don't know that anything can help you get back in, to tell you the truth. And I know that's a hard pill to swallow. But I brought you here to meet her so that you'd understand something. That place you're so desperate to break into? It's not the perfect home you think it is."

Cleo frowned. "What . . . what do you mean?"

Angie settled her arms over her stick, leaning heavily on it as she sighed. She cast a glance toward the house, then locked eyes with Cleo.

"Paige isn't from your building," the old woman began, her voice low and gentle. It reminded Cleo of Ms. VAIN. "She's from another."

"Another?"

"Yes. Up near Milwaukee," Angie explained, ignoring Cleo's puzzled look. "I used to live near it, in a place kind of like this one. Got food from its fields, worms from its compost, everything just peachy. Then something went wrong."

Cleo recalled Angie's first questions earlier that morning. She shuddered.

"Not sure what it was. A big storm? Computer glitch? Failure of some system or another? Anyway, the drones stopped working, inside and out, as far as I could tell. Fields not getting tended. Food not being delivered. From there, it was only a matter of time."

Cleo swallowed. "Time until what?"

"Until the inevitable. People were trapped. They tried to get out."

"Tried?"

"Some made it. I imagine most didn't."

"But Paige?"

Angie's brow furrowed, and she spat into the water. "Just a baby, for God's sake. Stumbling around outside, wailing to wake the dead. That's how I found her."

Cleo gasped. "All alone?"

Angie growled in reply. "Might as well have been. A few others managed to make it out—twenty or so that I saw. And not just kids. So I lead the poor little thing to where her people are huddled up, and what do they do? Hmm? They *run*. Imagine that. An old lady, trying to carry a little girl, both of us crying out for help, and they scatter like we're—"

"Like you're infected," Cleo whispered.

Angie nodded grimly. "Never did catch up to any of them. So I take this tiny creature back to my place, get her calm enough to tell me her name. I feed her, let her sleep, then try to return her in the morning. Maybe we'll get lucky, right? Find some young mother, desperate for her baby girl."

Cleo didn't need to ask how it went. The answer was hiding in the house behind her.

"We don't even make it out the front door. As soon as Paige hears we're going back to her building, she pitches the fit to end all fits."

Angie paused, rolling up her sleeves to show her arms to Cleo. Her skin was mottled with liver spots and moles, but among the splotches Cleo could see a series of dotted, oval-shaped scars. "Bite marks?" Cleo asked.

"Just so. I got these from trying to soothe her after I gave up on dragging her."

"Why did she—"

"Don't know. Don't want to know. But whatever it was that she experienced in that death trap, it terrified her so much she can't even stand to look at your building, much less get close to it. That's why I have to get the worms on my own. Paige is no help there."

Cleo's shoulders slumped. "That's why she ran . . . she's scared of me?"

Angie shrugged. "More scared of the idea of you."

"So she'll be no help getting me back in, either."

Angie reached out to rest a hand on Cleo's shoulder. "I'm telling you this because maybe getting back in isn't your best play, Cleo."

"But—"

"Your patient . . . your mom and dad . . . your world? I know. And I get it. But Cleo? That building isn't the sanctuary you think it is. It's not your world. It's not anyone's world." She stretched out an arm, sweeping it across the view of the lake. "*This is*. And it always has been."

"The buildings kept us safe! It's the only way we survived!"

"I survived!" Angie countered. "And not by cutting myself off."

Cleo found herself suddenly furious. "We had to! Influenza D—"

"Might have been cured within weeks, if people weren't so pigheaded! You don't know what you don't know, child. But I was *there*. I saw what happened when the flu hit. What do you think people did first, before anything else?"

Cleo clenched her fists but didn't respond.

"They got scared. Pointed fingers and screamed at each other. Built walls, all to keep it from spreading. It did anyway. Like it'll always do, because that's how the world works. So yeah, your apartments? A good plan, but a late one. Before that, it was years of denial and bickering and blame. We could've spent all that money and precious, precious time coming together, searching for a cure. But we didn't. Closed up and shut down instead, n' let the world chew on us, one bite-size piece at a time."

"We're safe inside," Cleo countered, but her voice caught on the last word.

Angie stared at her pointedly. When Cleo realized why, her cheeks prickled.

"Okay, so I'm not *inside*. But that doesn't mean the whole thing failed!"

"It rarely does all at once. Avalanches start with a single pebble. Hurricanes begin as a breeze. Earthquakes as a tiny tremble. When the world wants in, it gets in. Most of the time, you won't even see it coming."

"Well, if the world can get in, then so can I. I'm not giving up."

Angie shook her head and sighed. "No, I don't expect you are."

CHAPTER TWENTY-THREE

They finished their work in silence—or rather, Cleo did. Angie hummed as she baited the lines, growing louder when she noticed the way Cleo went pale at the squishy sound of the worms getting hooked. Cleo was no help whatsoever. She kept glancing back at the house.

"Looking for Paige?" Angie asked.

"Yes," Cleo replied softly. "Will she come out?"

Angie shrugged. "Gonna have to eventually. The outhouse is fifty yards down the hill."

"Are there any others?"

"What, outhouses?"

"People," Cleo murmured. She screened her eyes with her hand and squinted. The morning sun reflected powerfully off the water, but Cleo could still make out other buildings on the opposite bank. "Nobody lives over there?"

"Nobody *to* live over there."

Cleo shuddered. "So you and Paige are alone? In the middle of all this?" she said, gesturing toward the horizon. "It makes my head swim to even think about it."

Angie chuckled. "Better than being trapped inside. I knew from the get-go I couldn't handle it."

"Claustrophobia? It's an anxiety disorder that can cause dry mouth, sweating—"

"I know what it is. And you're not far off. A lifetime ago, before the flu hit, I did a stint in prison. That gave me a little taste of what it's like to be in a box. At least, enough to know it wasn't for me."

"You were in prison?"

"Yep!" Angie proclaimed, and she plucked at one of the rods. Its line sent ripples along the water. "Did a few dumb things, stole a few dumber things. 'Course now I can waltz in, take anything I want. Should've just waited ten years; could have got off scot-free."

"I've never met anyone who was in prison."

"Yeah, well, your sample size ain't exactly impressive."

Cleo couldn't argue.

Angie chuckled. "Paige and I . . . we, what? Double the number of people you've laid eyes on?"

"I've met lots on the simulator," Cleo replied. "But . . . yes. Paige is the first kid I've met for real, ever."

Angie grinned. "I don't know that you can say you've *met* her yet."

Cleo handed Angie her walking stick. "I'd like to, though. I didn't mean to scare her away."

"That would've happened anyway, once she got a whiff of you. Lord, child, but you do *stink*. Didn't notice it when we were back by the compost heap, but it's plain as day now. What did you do, roll around in it?"

Cleo scratched at her elbow. "Sort of?"

"Well, I've got soap in the house, and the solar panels on the roof still work, so I can heat up a bit of water for you. Nothing so grand as a bathtub, mind you, but it'll be enough for you to wash, at least."

Cleo sniffed at her shirt. Angie was right. She *stank*.

"Your clothes, too. And that blanket. We'll get you clean, maybe get a meal in you. Then we'll see if we can't get ol' Paige to come out of hiding."

"And you'll help me get back inside?"

Angie scoffed, "The soap? The meal? That *is* the help."

"But you said . . ."

"I said you were a smart girl, and that you'd figure it out once you'd rested and had some food. Don't think I'm so deaf I can't hear your stomach growling. Thought it was those stupid cats at first, but the sound followed me home, so I know it must be you."

As if on cue, Cleo's belly burbled noisily. Angie crossed her arms and smiled.

"Okay," Cleo mumbled, and she followed Angie inside, her pillowcase in one hand and Paige's stuffed dog in the other.

The back door of the house opened into the kitchen, and as soon as Angie swung it wide, Cleo could hear the patter of footsteps inside. She hopped several times, trying to see over Angie, but all she caught was a flash of yellow and green as Paige darted from the window. She had been watching them approach, Cleo guessed. A few seconds later, they heard a slam from down the hall to Cleo's right. Angie rolled her eyes.

"Like a chipmunk, that one."

"Chipmunk?"

"Skittish little rodent. Stuffs its cheeks with things, then runs. Paige is the same way," Angie said, and she propped her stick up against the countertop. A series of baskets sat along the counter, each filled with different kinds of fruits and vegetables. There were potatoes, carrots, apples, pears, corn, and spinach, along with several things Cleo didn't recognize. An old refrigerator dominated the far wall, its doors propped open by short stools. On the shelves were jars and boxes, arranged neatly and labeled: SALT. STRAWBERRY PRESERVES. VEGETABLE OIL. Cleo rubbed at her shoulder gently, feeling the muscles relax, slowly but surely. It felt good to be surrounded by walls and a ceiling again.

Angie kicked her shoes off onto a mat by the door and told Cleo to do the same. Cleo winced when she smelled her feet—they were even worse than her shirt. Angie noticed, too—she pinched her nose as she hustled to the stove. She turned a dial and grabbed a pot from inside the sink.

"Faucets don't work," Angie explained. "But I set up a rain catch a while back. One hot bath, comin' up.

Maybe a cleaner Cleo will help coax Paige out of hiding, yeah?"

Near the stove, a coil of hose hung on the wall, next to a big pitcher crammed full of long spoons, spatulas, and tongs. Cleo noticed that one end of the hose disappeared into the ceiling. Angie grabbed the other end and twisted the nozzle, then aimed it at the pot. Water trickled in—a meager stream at best, but enough to fill it after a few minutes. Cleo used the time to empty her pillowcase, arranging the contents on the counter and setting Yorick to guard them. He obliged by scooting forward and nearly ramming the basket of corn. Cleo had to catch him and put an empty basket over him to settle him down.

Once the water was hot enough, Angie set the pot on the back porch. She gave Cleo a big, threadbare towel, which she wrapped herself in before removing her clothes. They went piece by piece into the pot, until the water sloshed out onto the deck. Angie tossed Cleo's slippers in, too, and she even had Cleo try to get her silky blanket to fit. It didn't quite, but Angie seemed not to care; she popped back into the kitchen and reemerged with a box of powdered soap, dumping a generous amount atop the soaking pile. Then she used her stick to push the entire mound around, stirring it like a thick, lathery stew. Cleo huddled just inside the door, the towel draped over her.

"Going to need to rinse these in the lake. Fish won't mind, though. I do it all the time."

"I can take care of it," Cleo said, thinking about the old woman trying to lug her sopping clothes down to the lake with those twisted, swollen hands. She knotted the towel around her shoulders and hauled the pot to the lakeside. A shiver went down her spine as her bare feet sank into the mud, the cold of it squishing between her toes. *Never felt anything like this in the simulator,* she thought.

When she was done, Angie had her drape her clothes over the porch railing. "With this breeze, they'll be dry in a couple hours or so," she said. "In the meantime, I rustled up this old pair of sweatpants and a T-shirt. When you're done with your bath, you can have 'em."

A fresh pot of hot water was waiting for her on the stove, and Cleo took it back out to the lake, along with the box of soap flakes. It was a far cry from her shower at home, but by the time she was done scrubbing, splashing, and shaking out her hair, she felt cleaner than she ever had in her life . . .

. . . probably because she'd never in her life been dirtier to begin with.

When Cleo was done getting dressed and bandaging her still-sore hands and knees, Angie said, "Much better! And you even got under your fingernails. I do believe you just might be the daughter of a surgeon after all."

Cleo pulled a chair out from the little table in the corner. A blue vase sat at the center, and it held a single fake rose, dusty and cobwebbed. "I miss her," Cleo said softly.

"You'll get back there. Smart girl, remember?"

"But how do you get into a place that has no doors?"

Angie waggled her stick. "Food first. Then thinking. Trust me—brains work better after mashed potatoes."

Cleo raised a hand to object, but Angie had already started picking through the potatoes in the basket, and her stomach interrupted her with a furious growl. So she offered to help instead. Angie put her to work cleaning and peeling the potatoes.

"Where did you get all this food?" Cleo asked as she dug a blackened spot out of a particularly large tater.

"Paige."

"Paige?"

"That's right. She earns her keep by getting the food. Fields are pretty far from here—at least, for me. If you go up to the second floor and look out the back window, you can see 'em across the lake. Rows and rows, pretty as a picture. Fruit groves, too, and a greenhouse. There are scarecrows to deal with, sure . . . probably similar to your cleanser friends. But Paige knows how to avoid them, and the picker drones don't pay her any mind. She moseys over there for us once a week, grabs whatever we need."

"Sort of like our transport drones. We order our fruits and vegetables and protein, and they deliver it to us."

"Protein? You mean meat?"

Cleo shook her head. "Meat is a vector." doesn't eat meat

Angie rolled her eyes. "That makes sense. Too many diseases in pork and chicken. I'll tell you, I do miss a good steak, though. Not that I have the teeth to eat one!"

Angie cackled, and Cleo smiled, too. "But you eat fish?"

"Oh yes. Want to try some? I've got a few in the live-well. I could fillet one right quick, have it in the pan with a little salt and thyme."

Cleo shook her head rapidly, and she must have turned a shade white enough for Angie to let it go, because she murmured, "Right. Mash and greens it is."

"Th-thank you," Cleo replied.

Soon the kitchen was filled with the smell of boiling potatoes and vinegar, which Angie made herself. She had Cleo twist the lids off a few jars of pickled carrots and applesauce, too, and in just a little while, they had a lovely spread set on the table. Angie called out to tell Paige lunch was ready, but she received no reply.

"Eh," she said. "Kid's eaten worse than cold potatoes. Hers'll keep."

Cleo was ravenous, but she forced herself to take small bites, and to keep her elbows off the table. Midway through the meal, Angie got up and retrieved the sphere of calotexina florinase. She held it up to the window, letting the sunlight spear through it and cast a blue pattern on the floor.

"It doesn't make much sense, does it?" she said after a while.

Cleo swallowed another mouthful of potatoes. Her belly felt warm and round, and she could feel her mood changing already. It didn't bother her that Angie had picked up Miriam's medicine. Even a half-hour ago, Cleo had to admit, that would have driven her mad.

"What doesn't?"

"You said you had three of these?"

Cleo nodded and put down her fork. "Yes."

"They expire tomorrow?"

"Yes."

"And you got 'em a couple days ago?"

Cleo stood up. "I was thinking about that, too!" she exclaimed. "It was supposed to be a month's supply, but it wouldn't have lasted her longer than a few days, unless . . ." Cleo frowned. "Unless it's like you said, and the expiration date doesn't mean much."

"More likely these got tangled up in some technological glitch wilder than your hair. Who knows how long they bounced around before ending up at your door."

"You mean our tube. We don't have a door."

Angie shrugged and set the calotexina down. "Tube, door. Doesn't matter. Bottom line is someone messed up, whether it was a drone or the person who designed it. And you, poor thing, are left trying to fix that mistake."

"It feels like I've made a lot more than I've fixed."

"Isn't that the way of things?" Angie said, and she eased herself back into her chair. Cleo watched as she reached forward, carefully guiding her crooked fingers around the handle of her teacup.

"You have rheumatoid arthritis," Cleo said softly.

Angie took a long sip, then brought the cup to the table without setting it down. She squeezed her fingers around the porcelain until a few of her knuckles cracked.

"Have had, for decades now."

"Does it . . ."

"Hurt? Every minute of every day. I'd say I'm used to it, but something tells me you'd sniff that lie out pretty quick."

"If you were inside, my mom could take care of that for you."

Angie chuckled. "No, thank you. As long as I can bait a hook and hold my walking stick, I'm okay."

"Have you tried a glucocorticoid? If you took methyl-prednisolone, it could—"

"What? Now *I'm* your patient?" Angie snickered. "Trust me, kid. If it doesn't start with 'Band' and end with 'Aid,' I haven't heard of it."

Cleo arched an eyebrow. "That's not a valid treatment for rheumatoid arthritis."

Angie leaned back, resting her teacup on her belly and staring at Cleo. "How do you surgeons treat people, anyway? You can't see 'em, can't touch 'em."

"Surgical drones. We can view and talk to patients through them."

"But you can't actually be there?"

Cleo's head tilted. "No! If we were, we might spread infection!"

Angie stared at Cleo, who shifted uncomfortably in her seat.

"I . . . I'm just delivering the medicine. I wouldn't go if I was sick with anything."

"Oh, relax," Angie replied. "No influenza D for years, right?"

"But . . ."

The old woman smiled and closed her eyes. "Hey, for what it's worth, I think you're being noble." She ran the back of her hand beneath her chin, scratching at a few white whiskers. "You know, I used to like going to the doctor when I was your age. Sounds strange, but my doc . . . she was nice. Had the loveliest voice. And stickers!"

"Stickers?" Cleo said.

"Sure! Stickers, lollipops, little plastic spider rings . . . she had a whole basketful, and every time I went, I got to pick something out. If I got a shot, she'd let me pick twice."

"I don't understand."

Angie snorted. "It's like this: you can give me all the medicine in the world, but none of it is going to make me feel better like that basket of nonsense did. Or her voice. Or her gentleness."

Cleo's brow furrowed. Angie sighed.

"You fall when you were little, Cleo?"

"What?"

"Of course you did. Kid like you, throwing yourself on drones, tumbling around in the compost. Bet you took a spill or two, started hollering for Daddy and Mommy."

"Well, yeah, I guess."

Angie pointed at Cleo. "And what did they do?"

"They came to help me up."

"Did they slather you with medicine, give you a dozen shots? Drive a drone in your direction?"

"No! They hugged me and stayed with me until I stopped crying! One time, Dad grabbed his leg, too, and we spent the rest of the day limping around our apartment. We called ourselves the Kneebang Club, and he . . ."

Cleo trailed off, her lips pursed.

"See?" Angie grinned. "There's more than one way to fix a body."

Cleo only half heard her. She was still thinking about her mother and father.

"Maybe," Angie added, "that's why you're out here in the first place. Your doctoring instincts told you it was time to make a house call."

"Hmm . . . ," Cleo mumbled.

Angie flexed her fingers, which responded by popping angrily and snapping Cleo from her thoughts. "Anyway, I don't want you worrying about my hands. Use that big old brain to tackle your own problem, now that you've had a bit of food in you."

Cleo sat back, then shrugged.

"Let's start with what you know," Angie said. "That always helps me."

"You sound like Ms. VAIN. She takes good notes, and she recorded a lot of my trip. I could've just shown you . . ."

"Well, too bad. You don't have Ms. VAIN. You've got Old Angie. I make potatoes and listen well. Work with that."

Cleo closed her eyes. "Inside . . . it's . . . it's like a

living thing. The transport drones move just like blood cells through veins. And the units where we live—those are like the bones, right? The solid parts around which everything else moves. The network is the brain, I guess, and . . ."

Angie brought a hand to her mouth. Cleo thought she meant to cough, but instead she started chuckling, then laughing, then howling, banging a bent hand on the table so hard her teacup jumped.

"What?" Cleo crossed her arms and pouted. "It's how I made sense of it, anyway."

"You . . . ," Angie said, pausing to wipe a tear at the corner of her eye. "You sure that's the explanation you want to go with?"

Cleo raised her chin and set her shoulders. "Yes. I think it works."

Angie wiped again at her cloudy eyes. "S-sorry, kid, but you've tickled my funny bone."

"There's no such thing," Cleo responded glumly. "That's just your ulnar nerve."

Angie took several deep breaths. "It's an expression. Means you made me laugh."

"I can see that."

"Oh, come now, Cleo. Think about it. If that black behemothian building is a living thing, how do you suppose you got out?"

"I got dumped from the compost chute."

Angie grinned, her tongue visible behind the spaces in her teeth.

Cleo wrinkled her nose, but then a smile seized her, too. "Oh . . . ," she muttered. "Ohhh!"

She spent the next minute giggling. Angie was able to clear the table and return to her seat before Cleo was done.

"I think I owe you a bigger thanks for the soap," Cleo said, and she smiled again. But then, abruptly, her expression changed. Angie leaned forward.

"What do you know, kid?"

"That . . . that actually makes sense."

"The soap?"

"No. The compost. It's like the digestive system, right? The leftover waste comes out . . ."

"The living proof of which is sitting at my kitchen table."

"Which means there has to be a mouth—you know, some way for the fresh food to get in!"

Angie nodded slowly. "That's what the farms are for, yeah."

"So then there *is* a door. There has to be."

Angie shrugged. "Well, yes. But it's a hundred feet up, and on the north side of the building. The picker drones fly up there to drop off their loads." She paused, running a calloused finger along the edge of the table. Looking through the screen door and down at the pond, she murmured, "Good way to keep the infected out."

Cleo was on the edge of her seat. "And you said the picker drones don't pay any attention to humans . . ."

Angie squinted at Cleo. "Are you thinking what I think you're thinking?"

Cleo stood up and ran a hand through the impossible mane of her hair.

"I'm thinking I need to go upstairs . . ."

CHAPTER TWENTY-FOUR

Cleo and Angie stood at the base of the old wooden staircase. Light trickled in from a window on the landing, illuminating cobwebs and a thick layer of dust on each step.

"Paige went up there once. Ran back down crying, said it was dark and scary. I can't even get to the landing anymore," Angie admitted. "My knees won't let me. I can barely handle the porch steps as it is."

"I've never been up a staircase, period. Saw one in a game once, though."

Angie patted Cleo's shoulder. "One step at a time, and hold the banister—that's the handrail along the side."

Cleo nodded and set her foot on the first step. Little plumes of dust shot out to either side of her foot, and a spine-tingling creak echoed through the house, as though the old place was stretching awake after an eon of sleep. Cleo glanced back at Angie nervously.

"Nothing to worry about. They built these places sturdy." To demonstrate, Angie poked her stick at the step, which responded with a satisfying thump. Cleo smiled, and she grabbed the banister.

Hanging from the wall to her left was a series of pictures. Cleo paused at one, reaching up to wipe a layer of dust off the glass. Beneath was a photo of the lake, the trees surrounding it a gorgeous spray of reds, oranges, and yellows. An old man, wearing a floppy hat and a vest of many pockets, stood next to a boy, who beamed as he held up a fish on a string. The next photo revealed the same two people, joined by many more on the porch. Cleo peered at them.

"Are any of these you?" she asked.

"Doubt it, since this isn't my house."

"Oh," Cleo responded softly. The last picture before the landing showed the boy again, with a man and woman. Cleo recognized them from the middle picture; they had been holding the boy's hands. This time, the boy was perched atop the man's shoulders. The woman held a shaggy-haired brown dog. Cleo couldn't help but reach up and glide a finger along their forms. The dust came off in a line, revealing their smiles.

Cleo felt a sudden tightness in her chest. She wondered what her parents were doing. How worried would she be if her mother disappeared suddenly? It made her wish she had been kinder, or that she'd left a note—something, anything to tell them where she had gone.

Cleo pulled back her fingers, squeezing them into a fist at her side. She took a deep breath and kept climbing, around the landing and higher, up out of Angie's sight.

At the top of the stairs was a quiet, dark hallway. A faded rug ran along the center of the floor, drawing Cleo's eye to a room at the very end. She stepped carefully. Downstairs was obviously Angie's space. It was cluttered with the needs of the present—food and tools and blankets and books. Up here, though, was a still space. A memorial. Cleo thought she could understand why Paige had found it unnerving—there was no way to describe her urgent need to tiptoe, to pause at each picture and at each half-open door so that she could imagine the family from the photos lingering in those doorways, or straightening those pictures, or sleeping in those rooms. There certainly wasn't any internal organ that caused these sensations. She just felt them, and let herself feel.

The final door along the hall opened onto a bedroom. It was suffused with light, for a massive bay window took up most of the far wall. A set of yellowed lace curtains was drawn back to allow the sun to stream in. Just beneath the window someone had tucked a bench, and against the wall to her right sat the biggest bed Cleo had ever seen. It was a four-poster, covered by a beautiful canopy of red velvet. Dust had settled along the top, muting the color, but from underneath the scarlet was as vibrant as ever. The sheets of the bed were rumpled and one pillow was missing, but the bottom two corners of the bedspread were tucked neatly. Cleo ran her hand along those sheets, rubbing the dust from her fingers as she passed.

On the opposite side, next to the window, she noticed a table. Its surface was dominated by little bottles of orange plastic. She brushed the cobwebs away from their tops and picked one up. It was a container of medicine, or used to be: it, and all the others, was empty. Cleo glanced back at the bed.

Someone had been sick here. Very, very sick.

And someone had been a caretaker.

Cleo set the medicine bottle back into place, making sure its circular bottom fit the ring of dust perfectly. Then she moved to the window and gasped.

The view was staggering. Just past the lake and a low line of trees, Cleo could see the fields. They went on for miles, it seemed, another dizzying distance that only appeared to fade, rather than end. And it was all so bright, and so green!

Buzzing around in the rows of crops were the drones— hundreds of them. Cleo couldn't make out which types were which, but she could tell they came in all shapes and sizes. Some even rolled along the ground like the hippo drone she'd seen at the compost heap, following a pathway of brown that snaked its way through the fields. Cleo traced that route to a glittering dome. She recognized it as a greenhouse; there was one pictured on the seed packets her father sometimes received. And farther than that? Almost where the sky seemed to meet the ground? There were shapes: squares and rectangles, as perfectly formed as the sheer black structure of her own home.

Home, Cleo thought, and she squinted down at the fields again.

It took a few minutes, but one of the drones finally launched itself higher than the others. It didn't wander up and down the rows, but rather shot forward rapidly, following the dirt path in the opposite direction of the greenhouse. Cleo pressed her face to the window to try to follow it, and when it disappeared from view to her right, she hurried out of the bedroom and into the next room down the hallway—a bathroom. She had to stand on the toilet seat to be able to reach the window and look out, but she caught sight of the drone quickly. How could she not? It was easily a hundred feet above the rest, speeding along the horizon line. She couldn't see her building from Angie's house, but she was sure that the drone was headed in the right direction—the same she had come from that morning.

"This is possible," Cleo murmured, and she hopped down.

Angie was waiting at the bottom of the steps, a strange sack at her feet.

"Find what you were looking for?"

Cleo nodded. "Yes. The pickers must go to my building. I just have to be on one when it does. You were right!"

"Always am," Angie chuckled.

"Can I help you carry that?" Cleo asked, pointing down at the bag on the floor.

"Help me? It's yours," Angie replied. Cleo arched an eyebrow. She didn't recognize the buckle-and-strap-covered thing. She picked it up by a cloth handle.

"Backpack. Old, but good. And a darn sight better than that pillowcase you've been lugging around. I took the liberty of wrapping your medicine in a dishrag, then shoving it in an old soup can. Should protect it pretty well. Here."

Angie showed Cleo the shoulder straps, along with a clipping line that wrapped around her waist. A few quick tugs had the pack fitting snugly on Cleo's back, and she marveled at how comfortable it felt, all while keeping her hands free.

"Put some other things in there for you, too: your old clothes, your blanket, and your bony friend."

Cleo smiled. "Did he put up much of a fight?"

"Heck no. I opened the bag, and he just moseyed right in. Nearly dumped the whole thing on the floor."

"That sounds like Yorick," Cleo said.

"Refilled your water bottle and peeled some carrots. Also gave you a few pears and a jar of pickled beets. I know you're aiming to get that medicine delivered on the quick, but it'll take you an hour at least to walk to the fields, and there's no telling how much longer it'll be once you're back inside."

"Thank you so much, Angie! This is . . . this is amazing. I can't repay you . . ."

"Oh, I wouldn't be so sure . . ."

"Anything. Just name it."

Angie cleared her throat. "To tell you the truth, I didn't bring you here just to feed you, and getting worms wasn't really what I wanted your help with."

Cleo thought for a moment, then nodded. "Paige . . ."

"It's getting to the point where I can't do what needs doing around here. My knees, my back, these hands . . . At first I thought I'd be the clever old lady, convince you to stay on with us."

Cleo's face darkened.

"Don't worry. Gave up on that idea as soon as I saw how serious you were about this Miriam lady. But then I thought, 'Nice girl like Cleo? Another kid? Maybe she's just what Paige needs to get over her fear.'"

"So you want me to . . . what?"

"Well, you'll have to talk to her anyway—you're not getting past the scarecrows without Paige, and that's a given. If you can coax her out, it's a win-win for both of us. You get the help you need, and I get to say 'Cleo came from the building, and she's okay' next time we have to get worms. Might not work, but I figure it's worth a shot."

Cleo mulled it over for a moment, then nodded.

Angie smiled and reached up to ruffle Cleo's hair, which had dried into a massive cloud of curls. "Thatta girl," she said. "Now all you need is some way to get through to

Paige. She can be even more stubborn than me, if you can believe it."

Cleo narrowed her eyes, tapping a fingernail on her teeth as she glanced into the kitchen. The stuffed dog sat near the door, its floppy, shredded ears held on by a shoelace wrapped around like a headband.

"What's the name of Paige's dog?" she asked.

"Sweet mercy . . . you're asking me? She's got dozens of 'em."

"But that one?"

Angie scratched the side of her head. "Lord, um . . . Rowsby? Rottweiler? No! Wait! It's Rutherford!"

"You're sure?"

"Sure as I'm gonna get."

Cleo nodded. "Then I have an idea."

CHAPTER TWENTY-FIVE

Paige's door was at the end of a short hallway. Cleo could see light trickling from the crack underneath, and every so often a shadow would dance along the gap. When she got closer, Cleo heard the skitter of the girl's bare feet on the floorboards. It made her mindful of her own steps, and when the floor gave a particularly loud groan beneath her, she winced.

The skittering stopped, too.

Sighing, Cleo came down from her tiptoes and walked right up to the door. Rather than knocking or shouting, she simply sat down, putting Rutherford on the ground in front of her and the box Angie had given her to her right. Then she popped the catch on the box. Cleo had no idea why Angie had called it a tackle box—she didn't think that leaping at fish and trying to wrestle them to the ground was an effective way to catch them—but it was full of lures, hooks, and fishing line, just as Angie had promised. Making sure she had what she needed, Cleo took a deep breath, smiled at the old stuffy across from her, and began.

"Hello, Rutherford!" she declared brightly.

The dog didn't respond . . .

. . . which allowed Cleo to hear the soft gasp from behind the door.

"My name is Cleo!" she continued. "I come from inside."

Again, silence from Rutherford, but one wouldn't have known it by Cleo's reaction.

"Yes—exactly. From inside *there*. Oh. Paige has talked to you about it? She says it's really, really scary? And that's why she dropped you?"

A soft thump, as of someone slipping to their knees.

"I'm sure she didn't mean to! And it's totally understandable. I got scared recently, too, and I dropped something incredibly valuable to me, just like Paige. Only what I dropped? It broke. I'm so very glad you didn't!"

A brief shuffle, and the light beneath the door dimmed, blocked by something just beyond.

"I can't help but notice that you do look hurt, though, Rutherford. All those rips and tears! Why, I can see your stuffing at your belly, and both of your ears have come clean off! That can't be comfortable. What? Oh, yes, I'm sure Paige knows, and I bet she'd do something about it if she could. All good stuffy owners want that. Like me, for instance. My favorite friend inside is my elephant, Elly. She's gotten lots of rips . . . and some were even my fault."

Another quiet gasp, this one from right behind the crack.

"But I knew just what to do. Yep! Because I'm training to be a doctor. A surgeon, really. We help people feel better. I'm supposed to take a big test on all my studies in just a few days, but I found out that someone needs me even more than I need that test. That's why I'm out here—to help her. And I could help you, too, if you want. It wouldn't hurt a bit, and it would make it much, much easier for Paige to play with you and take you everywhere, just like I did with Elly, or just like I do with my silky blanket and my new friend, Yorick. You'd like him. He's funny."

A tiny voice whispered, "Yorick . . ."

Cleo took a deep breath.

"Nothing to worry about, Rutherford. Nobody sews like a surgeon. And I've got everything I need right here."

Reaching into the tackle box, Cleo retrieved the smallest hook she could find. Using a pair of pliers, she flattened the barb at the end of the hook, then did the same for the eye, squeezing it until it was just barely wide enough to take the fishing line. With steady fingers, she tied the coil of line off on the hook. Then she gently picked up Rutherford.

All told, it took forty-five stitches to repair the old brown dog, but Cleo was pleased with her work. She had even managed to reattach both ears. A pocketknife in the tackle box sported a pair of scissors, and Cleo used them to delicately snip off any poky bits of the fishing line. Then she ran a hand over Rutherford's belly.

Soft and smooth.

"There you go! All patched up and ready to play! What? Oh, yes, I know you're eager to show off your repairs to Paige, but we should give her time. She'll come out when she's ready. And there's no need to thank me."

Cleo brought Rutherford up to her face and made a chorus of licking noises.

"Ha! Please, Rutherford! I said you didn't need to thank me! But I suppose . . . if you insist, you *could* do me a favor. You see, I have to get back inside to save my patient, but Angie says there's no way I can do it . . . at least, not without Paige. There are these things called scarecrows, I guess, and I don't even know what they are, much less how to get past them. Paige is the biggest expert in the land, though. If you could ask her what to do, I'd be very grateful. Could you do that? Oh, thank you, Rutherford!"

Cleo set the dog down by the doorframe. She closed the tackle box, stood up, and said, "That's that." Then she walked down the hall, making sure her feet fell heavily on the floor. When she reached the corner, she dipped behind it and peeked.

Ten seconds passed.

Paige's door opened.

It was only a few inches—just enough for a hand to shoot out and grab Rutherford. Then the door slammed closed again. Cleo strained to hear, and she thought she detected a high-pitched squeal.

She hoped it was a happy one.

Cleo waited another five minutes, watching the shadow

bounce back and forth beneath the door. She began to wonder if her plan had worked.

But then the door opened again.

Cleo braced herself, ready to finally meet Paige face-to-face.

Instead, that slender hand snaked out, depositing the head of a teddy bear on the ground. It was the sorriest thing Cleo had ever laid eyes on.

At least, until its beat-up body joined it a few seconds later.

Cleo put a hand over her mouth to stifle her giggle, and she slid the tackle box back into place as she hunkered down next to the door once more.

"And what's your name, Mr. Bear?" she asked cheerfully.

After a few seconds, she heard, "Ichabod."

"Well, Ichabod . . . we've got some work to do!" Cleo declared, and she scooped up the head and body.

Seven stuffies later, the door finally opened wide. Cleo stood up slowly, holding out her hands to show that she meant no harm.

Paige stepped into the light. Her arms were stretched around eight recently repaired friends.

"Hey," Cleo said softly.

In a quiet, sure voice, the little girl replied, "You wanna see my room?"

CHAPTER TWENTY-SIX

There must have been a hundred treasures for Paige to present. Collections of curious stones. Bundles of dried flowers, brittle and beautiful, hanging from the window rails. Shelves lined with well-loved books, stacks of old photographs, and scraps of cloth. There were drawings of leaves and piles of blocks and heaps of laundry.

And everywhere, everywhere, the stuffed animals.

Paige had named each one, and each received a grand introduction, along with a detailed list of injuries the "doctor" could address once she had time. Cleo hummed and nodded at all of them, then offered a diagnosis and potential solution. Paige invariably repeated what Cleo said before setting the toy in its place of honor. "Dorsal laceration. Yeah," she'd murmur. "That's what I said when I found her."

Cleo smiled, and she wondered if this was what Angie had meant by spider rings and stickers.

description of paige

As the objects kept coming, Cleo found her attention drawn not to the things, but to Paige herself. Her skin was deeply tanned, and it was peeling along her shoulders and upper arms. Her hair—what little of it was left—was erratic and stubbly, thin enough to show a latticework of tiny scars on her scalp. Similar patterns were visible across her arms and the backs of her hands, and her legs were much worse. The bright green-and-yellow sundress the girl wore was cinched by a thin belt around her waist and stopped just above her knees, revealing thick scabs on both joints. And her shins? They were covered in bruises, cuts, and bumps. Some of them reminded Cleo of the itchy bites along her own calves, and she couldn't help but scratch at them as she thought.

"And this is Princess Wart. She's a toad," Paige declared, popping a brown-and-green toy onto the bed, right next to where Cleo sat. "At least, I think she is. She's missin' an eye and doesn't have a mouth. She might be another dog or something, but she looks toady to me. What do you—"

"Are you sick, Paige?" Cleo asked.

The little girl scowled, pulling Princess Wart tightly to her chest.

"No. I'm fightin' strong. That's what Angie says."

Cleo smiled softly. "I didn't mean to upset you. It's just . . . you've got some, well . . . what look like burns on your shoulders, and your hair . . . Inside, there are people who get very, very sick, and sometimes, the way we treat them can make their hair fall out. That, along with all your hurt places . . ."

Paige's nose, which was already short and flared to begin with, scrunched even further. "Well, that's not me. Angie cuts my hair like this whycause she can't use scissors much anymore, and I was all the time getting ticks. My shoulders are all peely from the sun. Angie says I should wear long sleeves, but it gets too hot and sweaty."

"And your knees?" Cleo asked, pointing.

Paige's face brightened, and she hopped up onto the bed. She bent her legs so that both knees were right below her chin, and then she pointed at the left one. "I got that sliding down a tree I climbed to get Angie's new walking stick. I went too quick and it got all scraped up. This other one was on a rock or log or somethin' in the lake. I was swimming and didn't even feel nothing, but when I came out it was all bloody. Angie said a shark bit me, but that's dumb because there's no sharks in the lake."

"So the bumps are just . . ."

"Skeeto bites. You got some, too."

"All this comes from . . . being outside?"

Paige nodded proudly. "Outside is the best place to be. Inside is scary, 'cept in my room where my stuffies can protect me." The little girl paused, her eyes fixed out the window. Cleo thought she saw Paige shiver, though she couldn't be sure. After a few moments, Paige added, "I don't like being alone."

Cleo recalled her own ordeal in the hallways. Had Angie said the power had gone out in Paige's building? Imagining a three-year-old by herself in those corridors sent a chill down Cleo's spine, and she knew better than to press the issue. Instead, she said, "Neither do I, which is why I have to get back to my family."

"And fix that lady, right?"

"Yes. That's why I need your help—I'm not as good at the outside as you are."

"It's scary to you?"

"Regular city mouse and country mouse, you two are," Angie said. Both girls turned to look at her. She leaned casually against the doorframe.

"How long have you been listening?" Cleo asked.

"Long enough to see your plan worked. Got some magic in you, Cleo."

Cleo blushed. Paige jumped off the bed.

"Angie, what's 'city mouse and country mouse'?"

"Old story."

Paige tugged at her sleeve. "Could you tell it?"

"Don't remember much of the details."

"Please?"

Angie nodded and shuffled over to the bed to sit by Cleo. Paige grabbed Princess Wart and flumped on the floor. Angie cleared her throat. "There's these two mice—cousins or sisters or some such."

"What were their names?" Cleo asked.

Angie picked up Rutherford from the side of the bed

and regarded Cleo's handiwork. "Not sure they had names," she said after a moment of thought. "At least, none that I recall."

"Can I name them?" Cleo asked.

Angie shrugged.

Cleo grinned. "Mudtoe and Lady Gumpish."

Paige squealed with delight. "Yeah! Mudtoe and Lady Gumpish!"

Angie groaned. "You've got to be the weirdest kid in your entire building."

Cleo held her chin high. "Except I'm not in my building, am I?"

"Well, you're the weirdest kid out here, too," Angie declared. Paige giggled. Angie sniffled and said, "So anyway, Lady Gumpish gets this letter from Mudtoe—"

"Yay!"

"—asking her if she wants to come visit in the countryside. Lady Gumpish hustles out there, and she has a simple lunch with her cousin or friend or whatever. Since she's from the city, she thinks the food is bland and Mudtoe's whole life is dull. 'The city is where it's at,' she proclaims, and she invites Mudtoe out there the next week."

"The city is where what's at?" Paige murmured.

"Everything. Excitement. Fun."

"Sounds interesting," Cleo said.

"Oh, just you wait. Mudtoe catches a ride into the city, and Lady Gumpish shows her this amazing spread of food. It's grander than anything Mudtoe has ever seen. Trouble is, it doesn't belong to Lady Gumpish. It belongs to the humans she's living with . . . and their big old cat. Right as those mice start feasting, the cat leaps at them."

Cleo shuddered. "I've seen what that's like."

"And either one of 'em gets eaten up, or they both barely escape. I disremember which. Anyway, Mudtoe says, 'You can keep your fancy, thank you very much. I'll stick with my piece of corn, thimble of water, and not being dead.'"

"Do they ever visit each other again?"

"No clue, but that's not the point. The moral is that the grass is always greener on the other side. Or, wait . . . one man's trash is another man's treasure? Something like that."

Cleo beamed. "I think I get it. People have different definitions of what makes a home."

Paige nodded knowingly. "Yeah, that," she added.

"And speaking of which," Angie concluded, lifting herself with great effort off the bed, "it's time we got you back to yours, Cleo. It'll take you two an hour to get to the fields, and Paige another hour to get home, and—"

"And I can't be out past dark, that's why," Paige announced.

"Yep," Angie agreed.

Out in the hallway, as they waited for Paige to gather her "explorin' stuff," Angie rummaged in a closet. "Got one more thing for you," she said. "Didn't want to put it in your backpack, though, on account of it might be useless."

The old woman pulled a slim gray case from the top shelf. Unzipping it, she slid out a tablet of black plastic.

"Had this old thing forever. I played games on it for a while, until my fingers . . . well, you know. It doesn't connect to anything out here, but maybe once you're back in, you can get your Ms. VAIN to fire up?"

Cleo took the tablet in both hands, holding it carefully. It seemed much more fragile than her scroll.

"Turn it on with that button there," Angie advised, and Cleo pressed it. The screen flashed blue, then white, and a loading bar appeared. When it was done, a bright mountain scene covered the surface, along with a few icons. Angie pointed to the top of the screen, where Cleo read **No Network Connection.**

Cleo turned it off quickly, not wanting to waste any of the battery charge. She nestled it back into its case, thanked Angie again, and slid the tablet into her backpack.

"There's a spot in the middle made for it. Second zipper from the front," Angie said, and patted the top of the pack once she had it closed.

Cleo turned to face her and smiled. Paige scampered down the hall wearing a pair of tightly laced sneakers. She had a backpack like Cleo's, and Rutherford was tucked underneath her right arm. "C'mon, Cleo!" she chirped. "Gotta go! Picker drones don't fly at night, 'cause that's when the sprinklers turn on!"

Cleo followed her into the kitchen, watching as she burst out onto the back porch and hopped down the steps. Cleo hesitated, though.

"Angie?" she called, turning around.

"Yeah?"

"Thank you," Cleo said, and she wrapped her arms around the old woman, burying Angie's face in an explosion of curls. Angie's hand patted the back of Cleo's head, and then she pushed her away.

"Remember what I said, kid, about the world getting inside. I meant it."

"Yes, I know. And I understand. But I've got to help Miriam and get back for my test and let my parents know I'm okay. Hurricanes and earthquakes and avalanches? Those are too far away. I can't worry about them right now."

Angie smiled. "The pebble never does," she said, and she nudged Cleo out the door.

CHAPTER TWENTY-SEVEN

"This is a scarecrow," Paige said, squatting by the side of the path and dragging a stick through the dirt. Cleo bent over beside her, trying to catch her breath.

"How . . . can . . . you . . . run . . . like . . . that?"

Paige shrugged. "I run everywhere. You're gonna have to run, too, to beat the scarecrows."

Cleo got her water bottle from her new backpack and took a gulp. Then she watched Paige draw. It wasn't much more than lines and circles, but it was enough for Cleo to recognize.

"That's a cleanser drone."

Paige shook her head. "Nuh-uh. It's a scarecrow. They're big and noisy and they really don't like it when you go in the fields, 'specially if you get close to the pickers. That makes 'em mad."

Cleo winced as Paige drew what looked like blades on the ends of the drone's spindly arms.

"How big are they, Paige? About the size of that log over there?" Cleo pointed into the woods. An old, crumbling tree stump looked to be about the size of a cleanser drone.

Paige squinted, then laughed. "No, silly! That's way too small!" she said. Then she scribbled a little stick figure into the ground by her sketch of the scarecrow. The spiderlike drone was easily ten times the size of the figure . . .

. . . which Paige was currently embellishing with a huge mop of curly hair.

"I think I get the point," Cleo said, and she swallowed nervously.

"'Kay!" Paige replied, and she took off again, Rutherford's ears flapping in the wind.

Cleo puffed out her cheeks and gave chase. Not a single one of her dance classes, not a moment in the simulator, had prepared her for something like this. She found it exhilarating to push herself forward, to churn her legs like Paige did and to experience what it was like to sprint headlong, no walls to crash into or corners to turn. And there was most certainly a difference—infinite differences, really—between running in the simulator and running here. It was the ground, with every step subtly unique. It was the way colors blurred at the edges of her vision. It was the way her body responded, lungs greedy and arms pumping and heart racing.

She found she could only keep it up in short bursts, and Paige had to circle back every few minutes to cheer her on. After their longest stretch, which took them over a bridge that crossed a small stream, Cleo held up a hand.

"I . . . I think I might throw up," she admitted, and she veered toward a patch of thick green-and-red leaves. Paige grabbed her by the backpack.

"Not there. That's poison ivy," she said. Cleo pulled back just before wading through the densest spot, and she fell onto her bottom on the dusty path. Her head was swimming, so she put it between her knees and concentrated on breathing.

"Yeah. If you thought your skeeto bites were bad, just wait until you have poison ivy. I got it once on my tummy and legs and arms all at once, and Angie made me roll around in the mud to keep from itching."

"Did . . . did it work?"

"Nah. I still scratched."

When Cleo had recovered a bit, she stared at the carpet of vivid plants. Paige said, "You gotta look at the leaves. If there's three, and they've got those little spiky parts, that's how you know."

"Thank you, Paige. You're very good at *outside*."

Paige thumped down on her bottom next to Cleo. In a whisper, she asked, "Are you good at *inside*?"

Cleo saw the fear in Paige's eyes. She smiled as softly as she could. "No. I'm terrible at it, actually. But don't worry—

I'm not asking you to take me to my building. Just to the fields. And you don't even have to go out there with me. You can stay in the woods."

Paige brought Rutherford up to her face, pressing his softness against her mouth. Her reply was muted by the dog's fur, but Cleo still understood. "You could stay in the woods, too. The scarecrows won't chase you if you're not in the fields. You'd be safe, 'n' you could live with me and Rutherford and Angie. We got space."

An image of the three of them, all sitting around Angie's table and enjoying a meal, snapped into Cleo's mind. It was entirely too pleasant, and it tugged at Cleo's heart in a way that unnerved her. Instead, she summoned that nightmare of Miriam on the floor, and another of her parents, sick with worry. Then she responded curtly, "No. I have to go."

Paige nodded, her wispy eyebrows arched and lips pursed. "'Cause you gotta help that lady," she said.

"Yeah," Cleo whispered. She could see the tears forming at the corners of Paige's eyes, and it looked like the little girl might bolt again. Desperate, Cleo added, "Oh, and Yorick!"

"Yorick?" Paige asked. Rutherford dropped into her lap as the girl straightened.

"I have to get him home! He has no idea what to do out here." Bringing her backpack around, Cleo reached in and felt the dome of the skull. In response, the tiny drone gave a whir.

"He's a bit . . . unpredictable," Cleo warned. Thinking of Angie's reaction, she added, "And he's kind of a skull . . ."

Paige leaned forward. "A skull? Like a dead one?"

Cleo shook her head quickly, but then nodded. "Sort of? He's actually an observation drone. Inside, he was buzzing around and bugging me . . ."

"Like a skeeto?"

"Yes, like a skeeto, only without the bites. So I took my model of a human skull and put it over him. It slowed him down, and now he's . . . well, I guess he's my friend, if that makes sense."

Paige rubbed Rutherford behind the ear. "Yeah. Makes sense," she echoed. "Can I see him?"

Cleo smiled and guided Yorick out. Paige gasped, but she didn't seem frightened in the least. In fact, she reached out to poke a finger through one of Yorick's eye sockets. She yipped when the drone inside vibrated at her touch, and she pulled back, awestruck and giggling.

"I'm going to let him go."

"Is he fast?"

Cleo shrugged. "Not terribly. I'm afraid he got a little banged up in our fight with the cleanser. Since then, he's been slow. Plus, I think he's missing the signals he'd get inside, so he'll probably just hover in place or fly straight ahead."

"Aww," Paige said. "It's okay, Yorick. Straight ahead is where we're going anyways!"

Sure enough, Yorick puttered down the path. Paige screeched gleefully and shot up after him. Fortunately for Cleo, the skull-bound drone wasn't nearly as quick as Paige, and the little girl seemed perfectly content to jog alongside the skull as it floated forward. Cleo followed behind, glad of the leisurely pace.

It was just as the day began to cool that Paige reached out and brought Yorick to a stop. Cleo packed him away again, then took a look around. In the distance, she could see a break in the trees. Paige pointed.

"That's the fields. I usually don't go that way. But you should."

Cleo peered through the foliage. It was hard to make out, but sure enough, her building rose in the background. She could see the sun beginning to set in the reflection of its solar panels.

"Thank you, Paige," Cleo said softly. "For bringing me here, and for telling me about the scarecrows. I'll—"

"You don't got rocks yet."

Cleo's head tilted. "Rocks?"

Paige nodded and curled her hand into a fist. "'Bout this big."

"Why?" Cleo asked, balling her own hand.

"You should run from the scarecrows. But if you can't, hit 'em in the face with rocks. Then run."

Cleo nodded gravely. "That's like our cleanser drones. I fought one, and when I broke its lenses, it flew off."

"Yeah. Maybe. You ever thrown a rock before?"

Cleo kicked at the ground until she unearthed one and then picked it up. It was sharp on her fingers and caked with dirt. "No," she said.

"You should try. Like this," Paige said, and she grabbed her own little stone. In one burst of movement, she hurled it at a nearby tree trunk. It thwacked off satisfyingly and left a little gouge in the bark. Paige stepped out of the way and added, "Now you."

Cleo set her jaw and dug her foot into the soil. With a snarl, she heaved the stone . . .

. . . straight over the tree.

"Uh-oh," Paige murmured, and she looked for more rocks.

For the next ten minutes, they practiced. Cleo never once hit the tree trunk, but Paige seemed pleased that she managed to get the stones moving forward, rather than up. "If a scarecrow is coming, it'll be way closer, so you won't miss as much," she offered helpfully.

Cleo sighed. "Thanks for the reassurance."

"You're welcome!" Paige replied, and she ran to the tree to gather up the rocks.

Once Cleo's pockets were bulging, they set off again, but they didn't make it far. Paige's steps slowed, and soon Cleo found herself alone on the path. When she turned around, she saw Paige standing about fifty feet behind her, clutching Rutherford and staring at the fields. Cleo's heart fluttered.

"Is this it?" Cleo asked when she doubled back.

Paige nodded.

Cleo took a deep breath. "Thank you, Paige. For everything."

Paige stared at the ground, then looked up slowly. "Cleo?"

"Yes, Paige?"

"Um, Rutherford says thank you, too. You know, for fixing him."

Cleo smiled and reached out to ruffle Rutherford's ears. "Goodbye, Rutherford," she said, "and goodbye—"

Before Cleo could finish her sentence, Paige spun and darted off, her shoes spraying dust down the path behind her. Cleo watched her disappear around a bend. A sudden throb of panic pulsed in her chest, just like when she first realized she had escaped her apartment, but she forced herself to turn around and face the fields.

"Right, Cleo," she whispered as she marched forward. "Get on with it."

CHAPTER TWENTY-EIGHT

The tree line broke onto a massive potato patch, a carpet of lush green dotted with bright purple flowers. Cleo rearranged the rocks in her pockets, putting four on each side. Their weight forced her to tie the drawstring of her sweatpants much tighter—she didn't want to be pantsless while staring down a scarecrow.

"All right," she whispered. "What now?"

Movement to her left drew her attention. In the distance, obscured by the glare of the setting sun, was a drone. It was large—Cleo could see that much. But whether it was a picker or a scarecrow, she couldn't tell. Just to be sure, she slipped a rock out of her pocket and juggled it with her fingers until it felt good in her hand. Then she stalked toward the drone.

About a hundred feet from her target, she could see what it was: a picker. Her eyes widened, and she crouched down in the vegetation around her. Angie had said that the pickers ignored humans, but she felt some primal instinct to be sneaky anyway. And from near the ground, she saw how the picker worked.

Four huge turbines held the drone aloft over a patch of potato plants. A long appendage, like a tail, curled underneath the drone. At its tip was a shovel, which it pressed into the soil around one of the potato plants. Once a plant was unearthed, two claws descended to ease it from the ground. A third grabbed the fully developed tubers and neatly snipped them off, depositing them into a belly-net just like the kind the cleanser drones had. When finished, the picker gently replaced the plant, patted the soil down around it, and unleashed a spray of water from a nozzle near its head.

Then it shot away.

"Wait!" Cleo cried, though of course it didn't. She stumbled and sprinted to catch up, nearly tripping when it suddenly stopped over another plant. It seemed to be looking for specific ones; maybe, Cleo thought, it could tell when the potatoes would be ripe. Before she could examine the plant it was tending to, though, it took off again.

Another twenty potato plants later, Cleo was panting. Sweat stung her eyes, forcing her to wipe at her brow with her sleeve.

"If this keeps up," she muttered indignantly, "I'm going to collapse before this thing goes home . . ."

It was time to be more aggressive, she thought.

After taking a sip of water, putting the rock back in her pocket, and making sure her backpack was closed and secure, she chased the picker drone to its next stop. With a deep breath, she walked right up to it. It didn't react at all.

"Okay, friend," she said. "You're loud and you're big. Are you strong, too?"

Wary of how her last attempt to ride a drone had gone, Cleo proceeded cautiously. She tried gently pulling herself up onto the drone's back, being careful to stay well away from its rotors. But before she could get a good grip, the shovel whipped down, nearly slicing Cleo's ear off on its way to the ground. Cleo tumbled backward, landing in a thick patch of plants. She growled as the picker hummed away once more.

Then she sat up, confused.

If it was flying away, why was it still so loud?

And why was the humming coming from behind her?

A simple turn of the head answered that question.

Paige was right: scarecrows were much, much larger than cleanser drones. They still leered ahead with a bank of glowing, glassy eyes, and their front plates were still surrounded by a halo of device-tipped arms. But they didn't have shovels or spray nozzles. Instead, they had blades, pickax heads, steel claws, and a crackling, two-pronged prod that filled the air with the burning smell of ozone.

And whereas the cleanser drones had a belly-net for capturing and releasing what they caught, the scarecrow's body was smooth and sleek.

Because, Cleo realized with a gasp, they didn't bother to capture their targets at all.

Desperately, she rolled backward through the plants. The drone rushed forward, extending all its arms in a fearsome mane around its head. They began to rotate rapidly, spinning so fast that Cleo couldn't tell one from another. The drone's eyes suddenly strobed with blinding lights, and it emitted a blast of deep, terrifying sound that shook Cleo's arms and rattled her rib cage. She screeched in response and dug heavy handfuls of dirt from the ground, flinging them into the drone's face.

It kept coming.

Scrambling to her feet, Cleo spotted the picker drone in the distance. She sprinted for it, each step tearing leaves off potato plants and kicking up more dirt behind her. Still booming, the scarecrow caught up to her with ease, and a long, blade-tipped arm shot to the right of her head. She dove to her left, coming up to her feet just as another blade scythed into the soil where she had been.

To her horror, the thing circled her, putting itself directly between her and the picker drone. Its arms started spinning again, and it roared.

She fled, darting to her right. But it was faster than she was, easily swinging around to hedge her back in. Those arms flew about, chopping at the air around her, causing her to scream each time they whistled past her skin. She was sure it would kill her any moment, and she closed her eyes, even as she kept moving.

It didn't kill her, however.

In fact, it didn't even touch her.

Cleo's legs were heavy, though, the rocks in her pockets banging against her hips and bruising her. And her lungs felt near to bursting. She was slowing down.

And then she stopped.

The monstrous drone lurched to a halt behind her, flinging its arms wide and bellowing at her again. But she had no wind left to run, and so she opened her eyes. She was just a few hundred feet from the tree line, and behind that, the path back to Angie's. She could make a break for it. She could sprint with everything she had left and reach the safety of the woods.

She could do it.

Which, she realized, was exactly what the drone wanted. For she wasn't being hunted—she was being *herded*.

With shaking hands, she reached into her pockets. The rocks felt jagged against her palm, and she squeezed them so tightly it stung her already-cut hands terribly. But it felt good to hold them, to bring them out and cock her arm back. The drone lashed forward with its pickax, sinking it into the soil inches from her feet.

Cleo fired a rock right at its face.

And missed.

"Go! Away!" she screamed, and she launched another rock. It sailed over the drone's head. She tried to pull out a third and fourth, but she was trembling so badly she dropped them.

The scarecrow rumbled closer.

Cleo shoved her hand into her other pocket, but the rocks there caught awkwardly against the fabric. She jerked and tugged, but they wouldn't come free.

So she froze.

The scarecrow loomed over her. It was earsplittingly loud, and it stretched its arms wide, then curled them around like the talons on a slowly closing claw. Cleo's hair whipped about in the updrafts created by its turbines.

Maybe it can't see me if I don't move. Maybe it can't see me if I don't—

It could most definitely see her. Almost delicately, it brought the topmost of its arms down. A sharp crackle and waves of heat pulsed from the prod. Cleo closed her eyes and held her breath.

It stabbed the prod into her shoulder.

Cleo's whole body jerked, and she was flung five feet away onto her backside. The scarecrow howled at her again and shot forward. She tried to tell her legs to move, but they wouldn't, and a huge claw, yet another of the thing's arms, clamped around her waist, pinning her own arms to her sides.

Then it started dragging her.

"No!" Cleo screamed, and promptly took a mouthful of dirt for it. The scarecrow was unrelenting, and Cleo scraped along the ground, her body digging a furrow into the soil. She felt little stones and the stalks of the potato plants cutting her as the drone plowed forward, and the force of it ripped her backpack right off. She twisted to try to glimpse where it had landed, but all she could see was the hideous thing that had her.

Until, quite suddenly, it didn't.

At the same time the claw disengaged, Cleo heard a sharp clang.

Then another.

And a high-pitched keen—the kind made by a little girl screaming at the top of her lungs.

Roaring in reply, the scarecrow sped off, leaving Cleo torn up and bleeding in the dirt. She winced at a million-million scrapes but forced herself up into a kneel.

Paige was there at the edge of the field, a pile of rocks at her feet. She held Rutherford in one hand and with the other scooped up rock after rock, hurling them at the scarecrow. A few sailed wide, but most cracked directly into its faceplate.

It barreled toward her, undeterred.

"Run, Cleo!" Paige howled, and Cleo staggered to her feet.

Only to fall face-first back into the plants.

Everything hurt. The prod had messed with her ability to communicate with her arms and legs. She could barely breathe.

But she had to *move*.

Again, she rolled up. Again, she told her legs to run. And again, she fell. But this time, she managed to scramble a few feet forward. Growling, Cleo pushed up a third time.

Shreds of leaves and clumps of soil fell from her hair as she turned to find Paige.

The girl was nowhere to be seen—a fact that terrified Cleo but only seemed to enrage the scarecrow.

"Paige!" Cleo shrieked as she willed herself to her feet. Her hands were still spasming, but she brought them up to cup around her mouth anyway. "Paige!"

Almost effortlessly, the scarecrow pivoted in midair, the sound of Cleo's voice giving it something new to menace.

And then Paige reappeared, popping out from the edge of the forest, more rocks in hand. She chucked them two and three at a time at the scarecrow, which swung about again to pursue her. As soon as it got close, Paige darted back behind the trees, only to sneak out another hundred feet in the opposite direction, slinging stones and insults at the thing until it took up the chase anew.

"Oh, clever," Cleo murmured.

"Go, Cleo!" Paige cried.

Cleo forced herself to leave Paige alone with the drone, spinning around until she spotted her backpack. It was nestled between two shredded potato plants. She dove for it, snagging it with one hand and coming right back up with the bag slung over her shoulder. Then she looked for the picker drone.

It had made its lazy way down the row of potatoes and was twice as far away as Paige and the scarecrow.

Cleo made a run for it.

Too busy with Paige, the scarecrow didn't follow her.

It didn't need to.

Cleo gasped as a second scarecrow flashed in behind her, closing impossibly quickly. Her legs wobbled with each desperate stride, and twice she stumbled, using her hands and running on all fours at times. Her wild movements sent up a spume of dirt and potato leaves behind her, peppering the scarecrow across its faceplate.

It slowed, just a little.

Just enough.

She reached the picker as it was taking off, its shovel-tail curled under and rotors out wide. Not knowing what else to do, she launched herself up at it, snarling her fingers in its netting. Its rotors began to whine with the effort, but it slowly lifted Cleo in the air. In a panic, she heaved herself upward, tangling her feet into more of the netting and holding on for dear life. Below her, the scarecrow slashed at the dirt, circling as it sought her out.

But she wasn't on the dirt anymore.

In fact, she was nowhere close.

Though the potato net to which she clung was mostly empty, the drone was ascending. Twenty feet. Thirty. Fifty.

My weight, Cleo realized. *It thinks it's full.*

Craning her head, Cleo scanned the ground for Paige. She wasn't visible, but the first scarecrow was hovering in place at the edge of the trees. She couldn't be sure, but she thought she saw one more rock fly from the depths of the woods, shattering one of the scarecrow's sensor lenses.

Cleo smiled and closed her eyes—the height was

making her dizzy, and she had to concentrate on clinging to the net. She was grateful that the picker didn't move nearly as fast as the scarecrow—it would have thrown her off as surely as the transport drones had. But she could tell from the way her hair whipped about that they were making progress. Another fifty feet higher and the drone leveled off. It glided through the air, a few potatoes and a twelve-year-old girl along for the ride.

CHAPTER TWENTY-NINE

Though she'd refused to open her eyes, Cleo could tell something had changed. The light that translated through her eyelids faded, and the wind died abruptly. The drone seemed much louder, too, and Cleo realized its humming was echoing off walls.

She was back inside.

When she looked, she saw that the drone was skimming low to the floor; if she let go of the net, she could have touched it. She tilted her head back carefully to glance behind her and saw the entrance. It appeared no bigger than a dinner plate, and it was shrinking by the second as they raced forward.

To where, she had no clue.

They did not pass hallways or apartments, even though they were certainly high enough to be in the middle of the building. And as the entrance faded out of sight, so did the light. The only clue Cleo had was that they didn't turn. By her estimation, the picker was taking her to the very center of the building.

It made sense, she supposed—store the food in the middle, where it could get to all the apartments easily. Someplace where the drones could collect it, deliver it, and easily return for more. *The heart*, Cleo thought.

And when the drone burst into a massive chamber, one full of light and noise and energy, she realized she wasn't far off.

The floor fell away beneath her, and a sudden cross breeze threatened to tug Cleo from the drone. She renewed her grip, wincing as her shirt shifted along her back, aggravating all the scrapes and cuts the scarecrow had given her. She could feel the fabric clinging, sticky and wet—probably with blood, she realized grimly.

"Nothing to be done about it now," she whispered, wishing there was someone who could hear her.

Besides, of course, the swarming menagerie.

Everywhere, drones zipped along—transports, repair drones, and hundreds of the little observers. There were no cleansers as far as Cleo could see, for which she gave quiet thanks. Gradually, her picker drone descended, lowering until they had nearly reached the floor. The beams of dozens of observation drones crisscrossed in the air, revealing to Cleo that they had reached a queue of some sort. The picker hovered behind six others of its kind, lurching forward only when the drone at the head had dumped the contents of its net onto a conveyor belt, where the crops were carried away through a darkened hole in the wall. Cleo thought it would be wise to let go before her drone deposited her on that same belt, so she disentangled her legs from the net and guided herself to the grated floor. Its pattern beneath her slippers sent a tingle of familiarity through her, and she breathed deeply for the first time since they'd entered the giant room.

She grimaced. Breathing hurt. Moving hurt.

And with every step, dirt seemed to cascade through the grating beneath her, trickling out of her hair, her pockets, her slippers, the seams of the backpack—she was filthy from head to toe. "Thanks for the bath, Angie . . . ," she mumbled ruefully, flinching as she felt the pack settle against another badly scraped spot. She quickly swung the backpack around and unzipped it. The erratic, swirling lights of the speedy little observation drones weren't enough to allow Cleo to make out much other than what was right in front of her, so she figured it was time for her grinning friend to reappear.

As soon as she had the top of the bag open wide, Yorick meandered out. Cleo expected him to stay by her side, but the tiny drone buzzed through the air, up and up and well out of her reach. She started to call out his name, but she slapped her hands over her mouth—the last thing she needed to do was attract the attention of a cleanser. Instead, she tried to follow his lights. They took her up an aisle of conveyor belts, each one apparently for a different kind of produce. She had to duck a carrot picker and sidestep a drone dumping rice into a funnel. Fortunately, it was easy to follow Yorick.

Mostly because she wasn't the only one doing so.

"Who's the anomaly now?" Cleo smirked. Yorick, wearing his skull helmet, had picked up an entourage of other observation drones, who trained their lights on him and traced his path through the air. He couldn't move nearly as fast as them, so by the time he descended, there was a swarm of twenty or more observers around him. As if exasperated, he glided back to Cleo, who plucked him out of the air and tucked him under her arm.

"Way to blend in," she teased him. He seemed to smile back sheepishly.

There was a hollow space beneath the frame of the closest conveyor belt, and Cleo crawled her way in. The crowd of observation drones hovered around the belt, their lights illuminating the little nook.

"Oh, shoo," Cleo snapped. "We're busy."

First up was assessing her injuries. Even with Yorick's light, she had to do most of the examination by touch, since the worst abrasions were painted across her lower back. Hugging herself, she walked her fingertips along her skin, gasping each time the pain arced up her spine. All told, she counted six really bad spots, all of them still bleeding, all still caked with dirt. Her hands, fingernails, and face were equally grimy, so she prepped herself for treatment the only way she could.

She used the rest of her water supply.

Even being as frugal as possible, cleaning her hands took half the bottle. The rest she reserved for her back. Angie had packed her pillowcase, washed with all the rest of her clothes, in the pack, and Cleo pulled it out reverently. She pressed her face into it and inhaled. It no longer smelled of home, but traces of Angie's soap lingered, and that comforted her, too.

"Thank you," she whispered.

And then she tore it in two.

One half she used to clean her wounds, wringing the sopped-up blood and dirt through the grating. The other half she shredded into strips, onto which she slathered the last of her antiseptic cream from the first aid kit.

Finally, she mummified her torso.

And she stifled a scream.

Pain sizzled along her back, the gluey cream burning out all the bacteria as it bonded with her skin. Cleo reached out and grabbed one of the conveyor supports, pressing her forehead to it until the stinging subsided. Then she waited another five minutes, afraid that any movement would cause the bandages to shift and the agony to start afresh. Only when she was sure that the wrapping had set did she dare to put away the first aid kit.

Or to see if she could conjure an old friend.

Nestling herself against the wall, the belt churning just above her hair, Cleo felt along the backpack for the second zipper. When she had the gray case in hand, she eased out the tablet and turned it on.

Cleo couldn't bear to look at first, so she made a mask out of her hands and cracked her fingers apart just enough to see the upper right-hand corner of the screen. When she read **Network Connection Established**, she allowed herself a quiet whoop of relief.

Trouble was, she had no idea what to do from there.

"Connect to VAIN," she whispered.

It didn't respond.

"Open dialogue box."

Nothing.

She glanced out at the floor around her, but she couldn't see anything except the bright lights of the still-swarming observers, and it was hard to hear much past the pop of pears hitting the belt above her. So she took a deep breath and declared, "User menu. Please."

Still nothing.

"Guess it doesn't respond to voice," she muttered to Yorick.

The icons that surrounded the image of a mountain were all new to her—or, she reminded herself, were all older than she was. Some were labeled as games, but others' purposes were less clear, and a few were total mysteries. Shrugging, she tapped one. It brought up a white box, kind of like a piece of paper, and an image of a keyboard. Cleo typed a few words, then hit enter.

The blinking cursor just moved to the next line.

Rolling her eyes, she closed that window and tried another. And another. And another. Finally, she tapped a boring-looking black square. A dark box, nearly the opposite of the first she had tried, popped up. She sighed when the keyboard appeared, but then her eyes widened. There, in the corner of the box, it said:

Network Interface. Command Prompt:

Cleo typed, "Connect to VAIN," and pressed enter. Nothing happened at first, but then a string of letters and symbols cascaded down the page, going so fast Cleo couldn't read them.

Then the black box disappeared.

And the VAIN interface filled the screen.

"Yes!" Cleo hissed. She kicked out with her feet rapidly and pumped her fists, which sent Yorick bouncing about inside the skull. "Oh, sorry . . . ," Cleo whispered. "I'll put you down if you promise not to fly off again."

Yorick didn't respond, but she put him down anyway. He rose a few inches off the floor and glided toward the edge of the conveyor belt, but he was met by a wall of observation drones, and he turned around, settling on the floor by Cleo's side. She smiled and turned her attention back to the screen.

Virtual Adaptive Instructional Network
Use Voice Recognition to Log On

Cleo frowned. "I can't use my voice. Or you can't hear it," she said.

She touched the screen. It brought up the keyboard, and she typed in her code. It didn't work, so she tried it again, this time with punctuation. Still nothing. She tried it all as one word, in all capitals, all lowercase.

All useless.

With a growl, she closed the keyboard window and stared at the blue letters.

She poked at them.

She shook the tablet.

She nearly tossed it at a random observation drone.

"C'mon, Ms. VAIN," Cleo moaned. "Help me out here!"

As if in reply, a little green cloud appeared in the lower right-hand corner of the screen. Inside, tiny letters informed her, "Your microphone is turned off. Adjust audio settings in the control panel."

"Now she tells me," Cleo grumbled. It took her another five minutes of clicking, swiping, and closing boxes before she found the control panel. From there, she just followed the icons—a speaker, a little smiley face with musical notes pouring out of its mouth, and finally a picture of a microphone. She toggled it on, then returned to the VAIN portal.

"Head, shoulders, knees, and toes," she said. She almost sang, but didn't want to risk it.

The soft blue letters faded, and a load screen came up. Cleo bit her lower lip softly. This never happened on her scroll. Then again, her scroll wasn't a technological fossil.

"Cleo, love? Is that you?" a gentle voice asked. A few

seconds later, a grainy animation of Ms. VAIN appeared. Cleo could've kissed the screen, she was so happy.

"It's me, Ms. VAIN! I'm back!"

"One moment, dear," Ms. VAIN said. She blinked a few times, then smiled. "I'm having a great deal of trouble accessing the cameras on your scroll, and the connection to the database is quite slow. Also, I'm reading some very strange graphics and sound settings on your end. Did your scroll get damaged?"

Cleo blushed. "Um, maybe? I'm not exactly on my scroll at the moment."

"Where are you?"

"I'm in the heart, I think. Here. Look."

Cleo turned the tablet to face the room. The observation drones all shone their lights on it at once.

Ms. VAIN said, "I can't see anything, love. The device you're using might not have a camera, or it might be disabled."

"You can hear me okay, though?"

Ms. VAIN nodded and reached up to tap her left ear. "Loud and clear."

Cleo sighed and pressed her forehead to the screen. "Thank you, Angie," she whispered.

"What's that, dear?"

"Angie. She's . . . a friend. She helped me find you."

"Was I lost?"

Cleo shook her head but then realized Ms. VAIN

couldn't see it. "No. I was," she said, and she quickly told Ms. VAIN about her time outside. Ms. VAIN listened patiently, nodding and praising Cleo for her wisest decisions.

"So what will you do now?"

"Explore, I guess," Cleo replied. "If this really is the heart, then the drones should be able to get just about anywhere in the whole building from here."

"That would make sense."

"And if they can, maybe I can, too."

"A sound theory, love."

Cleo rubbed at her temples. "Thanks. Now I just need to test it."

After a quick carrot break, Cleo packed up her bag and secured it on her back. She thought about slipping the tablet into its case, but she found she couldn't bear to put Ms. VAIN away, even though 20 percent of the battery life was gone already. Instead, she held the tablet in one hand as she crawled out from under the conveyor belt. Instantly, she was surrounded by observers, but Yorick head-butted his way through the wall of drones, knocking them to the side as if to say, *Back off. This one's mine.*

Cleo tried to creep along at first but gave up when the cloud of drones and their light beams cast her less-than-stealthy shadow on the wall in giant fashion. She passed more conveyor belts, watching as the fruits and vegetables disappeared into the wall, probably to be washed and prepared. And she looked up on occasion, too. There was no visible ceiling, just a chaos of drones dancing in a dizzying, crisscrossing column. Cleo decided to pick one at random and watch where it went.

The empty transport drone she chose seemed to spiral downward gradually, though it had to move in fits and starts as other drones zipped in front of it. Once it neared the floor, it skimmed away from her, forcing Cleo to venture farther into the middle of the cavernous room. The throng of observation drones only got thicker, until she was bathed in so much light that she couldn't see beyond them. And when she stopped, they crowded in so thickly that she had to reach up and part them like a curtain. They whined every bit as loudly as Yorick did pre-skull. Cleo stowed her tablet and covered her ears, but it barely helped.

"Leave us alone!" Cleo shouted, and she dashed forward suddenly, grabbing Yorick as she passed. Shielding her face, she crashed into a dozen of the drones. They were so light that they spun to the side with the impact, their lights strobing along the floor in Cleo's wake.

Just beyond the dome of drones, the room got much darker, and Cleo's eyes didn't have time to adjust. She zigzagged blindly, nearly stumbling into several of the lazy transports. Only when her head was throbbing with exhaustion did she stop. Fortunately, it seemed as though she lost most of the observation drones, though she could still see their beams sweeping around far behind her, their sensors scanning the space for a strange, girl-shaped anomaly.

Cleo let go of Yorick and turned him to face forward. His lights revealed that she was near another wall: the one opposite the conveyor belts. As she watched, the empty transport drone she had followed sailed right up to a hole in the wall. It swung about, aligning its empty frame with the space. Then it backed in and came to a complete stop. To her surprise, a dim red light began to glow just beneath its lenses. It pulsed slowly, rhythmically, almost like the breathing of a sleeping child.

It was then that Cleo noticed the rest of the lights: the wall was covered in them, spaced at regular intervals. Most were crimson like the first, but a few were green. None was even half as bright as Yorick's glow, but combined they made for a display that Cleo found quite lovely . . . and intriguing.

"I . . . I think they're charging," Cleo said. Yorick could neither confirm nor deny her suspicion, but he obliged her by floating forward. She followed him all the way up to the wall, where she saw yet more hollows. They were of many different sizes—some as big as the largest transport drones she'd seen, and some as small as, well, Yorick.

"It's like the honeycombing inside a bone," Cleo observed. Yorick turned to face her, and with his grin as wide as ever, tried to back up into one of the tiniest hollows. The skull was too large, though, and no matter how many times he rear-ended the opening, he wouldn't fit.

"Do you need to rest, Yorick?" Cleo asked him. He hovered there. Smiling, she snatched him out of the air, flipped over the skull, and fished the little drone out. When she held up her hand, he happily backed into the opening. His lights shut off immediately, replaced by a little red signal, just like his bigger brothers and sisters.

Cleo reached out and pressed a fingertip right between his lenses. "Just a few minutes, silly drone," she warned him. Then, worried she might not be able to find him again if she went exploring, she rummaged in her bag until she found another carrot. She shoved it into the gap between his eyes, where it stuck out like a ridiculously long nose.

"That's a good look for you," she giggled, and she crammed the skull into her backpack.

With her left hand gliding along the faceplates of the lowermost charging drones and her tablet tucked under her arm, Cleo began to trace the huge room. A few of the observers found her again, but as long as she stayed moving, they didn't overwhelm her. They actually helped— their beams sweeping behind her illuminated her path and allowed her to see a fair distance into the room. A flurry of movement to her right caught her eye, and she strayed from the wall to get a better view.

It was a vortex of drones, a swirling column that descended through a gaping hole in the floor. The ceiling was too high for her to see, but she assumed it had an opening, too, much like the space she had encountered when she had first left home.

Home . . .

How long ago that seemed, the moment she broke free of her tube! Cleo had to remind herself that it had only been a couple of days. And this cavernous space—never could she have imagined that something so large could be a part of her tiny world.

Only, she could hear Angie saying, this wasn't her world.

The heart seemed somehow grander and more imposing than even the sky above Paige's pathways, and Cleo found herself missing the warmth of the sun along her shoulders and in her hair. But she shook that longing off, reminding herself that it'd be even darker outside than the drone-brightened chamber she was in now.

"Ms. VAIN," Cleo asked, bringing the tablet up. "What time is it?"

"According to this device's internal clock, it's nine fifty-seven in the morning . . ."

"That can't be right . . ."

"On December 11, 2088."

"That's *definitely* not right."

Ms. VAIN blinked. The clock on the wall behind her shimmered for a moment, and then read a new time.

"There. I've synced your device with the database. It's eight thirty-two p.m. on May 27, 2096."

"Thank you, Ms. VAIN," Cleo replied.

"A reminder: your level-one surgical exam is in approximately sixty hours."

Cleo dodged out of the way of a pack of repair drones. "And Miriam Wendemore-Adisa's medicine might expire in less than five," she countered. "One thing at a time."

"Another reminder: if you fail the exam, you are not

permitted to retake it for an entire year. Further, two fail-
ures disqualify you from the medical track entirely."

Cleo gritted her teeth, glad her teacher couldn't see
her expression. "Thank you again, Ms. VAIN. I promise I'll study every single moment I can, *after* I help Ms.
Wendemore-Adisa."

"Of course, dear. In the meantime, would you like to
sing a song about the small intestine?"

"I really, really wouldn't," Cleo replied, lowering the tablet. Then she slowly backed away from the helix of drones.

A cleanser had appeared, rising out of the hole in the
floor and navigating between the much-slower transports.

When its many-eyed face had turned away from her,
Cleo scurried back to the wall. She retraced her steps until
she found the carrot sticking out of Yorick's cubby. As
quickly as she could, she yanked him free of the charging
station and stuffed him back in his skull. Then she looked
over her shoulder.

There were three more cleansers, their spindly arms
waving about. The observation drones clustered around
them, almost like they were whispering secrets. After a few
moments, the closest cleanser pivoted sharply. Its lenses
caught the dazzling reflection of the observers' lights.

All of which suddenly pointed at Cleo.

"Gotta go, Yorick!" she said, and she took off in the
opposite direction, the wall to her right this time. Again
she found herself mostly in the dark, and she didn't dare

turn Yorick around to light her path. Careening off transport drones, she bumped and battled her way along, pausing every hundred feet or so to look behind her.

The cleanser and its little henchmen were gaining on her.

With a gasp, Cleo scanned the wall. She couldn't see much, except for the red lights of the charging drones. That was enough to help her find what she was looking for, though. Spotting an opening farther down, she rushed toward the empty space, hunching over so she could fit into the transport drone's dock. Then she backed in and waited.

The cleanser passed her by.

Cleo exhaled sharply. Her first thought was to sneak back out into the heart and to keep exploring, but the observation drones were still too thick outside her hiding spot, so she turned her attention to her current space. The cubby was deeper than she'd expected. In fact, to Cleo's surprise, it led to another room, though one much smaller than where she had been. She brought Yorick up, and the light shot from the skull's eye sockets, revealing something that took Cleo's breath away.

The entire room was *moving*.

One more step and Cleo would have found herself on a river of rolling cylinders. Their hollow lengths bounced along from right to left, flowing into the room through a wide hole near the bottom of the far wall. They went around and around, forming a loop that took up most of the floor. Every so often, a huge robotic claw, attached to a swivel on the ceiling, swung down and grabbed one of the cylinders.

It reminded Cleo a little of Angie's fishhooks.

And a little of the scarecrow.

As Cleo watched, the claw brought a cylinder to a slot in the far wall. The end of the cylinder slid open, and something was pushed inside. A pattern of colorful lights blinked above the opening. Then the arm brought the cylinder back to the wall nearest Cleo, which was honeycombed just like its other side. The back ends of the charging transport drones were clearly visible in their cubbies, empty and waiting for new cargo. The claw seemed happy to oblige them; it carried the cylinder to a waiting transport and pressed it in, where it locked into place with an airy *whoosh*. A few seconds later, the transport drone took off, and another one slotted into its place to charge.

Cleo immediately recognized the cylinders as empty transport containers, the kind that the drones brought to the apartments and delivered into the tubes. Food came in them. Miriam Wendemore-Adisa's medicine had come in one. Heck, everything came in one of those tubes—including, according to her dad's story, people.

And that gave Cleo an idea.

She watched four more cylinders receive their cargo and get loaded into transport drones. Each time, those lights above the delivery slot flashed.

Cleo counted.

There were six of them.

So excited her breath caught in her throat, she watched the pattern of the next one: yellow-yellow-blue-violet-blue-red. That was followed by orange-green-green-green-red-yellow.

The number was right. The colors seemed right.

And Cleo? She couldn't wait to see if she was right, too.

CHAPTER THIRTY

"**W**ould you like to hear a story about a stowaway?" Ms. VAIN asked.

"What's a stowaway?"

"Someone engaged in the very plan you're proposing: to sneak into a form of transportation in order to travel. Most frequently, they use naval vessels . . . that is, ships . . . but there are also tales of people jumping on trains, hiding in the backs of automobiles, even slipping into the landing gear of an airplane before it takes off."

"Do any of them pack themselves in transport drone cylinders?"

Ms. VAIN blinked. "Shipping containers, yes. Cylinders, no. You're a regular trailblazer these days, Cleo."

"I'll pass on the story for now. I've got to figure out how to get up onto that claw . . ."

That was her plan: cling to the claw until it picked out

a large enough cylinder for her to ride in, then wait for one that was going to Miriam's floor. She'd drop into the open cylinder, toss out the delivery, and hitch a ride all the way up. Cleo supposed it was hoping for too much that the one she chose would be delivered directly to the right apartment, so she intended to break free of the cylinder once she was able. Then she'd walk to Miriam Wendemore-Adisa's unit and figure out what to do from there.

"Simple enough, right?" Cleo had said after explaining the plan to Ms. VAIN.

"If you say so, dear," her teacher had replied.

Of course, Cleo knew that no part of this would be simple, and especially not the first step. She had no idea what was below the rumbling cylinders, or if they'd support her weight, or if she could stay atop them long enough to even get to the claw. She rooted around in her backpack and found the jar of pickled beets.

"I guess this is kind of like my foot . . . ," she said. Yorick smiled. Ms. VAIN couldn't see the jar, but she nodded comfortingly.

Cleo lowered herself to her stomach at the edge of the drop into the cylinder chamber. Reaching down, she let the rolling containers brush against her fingertips as they moved past. They weren't spinning particularly fast, but the movement was constant, and she noticed that those that didn't get picked went around the room again and again, waiting their turn. As gently as she could, she set the pickled beets onto one of the cylinders.

Then she let go.

The spin of the first container flipped the jar over, but it didn't break. Instead, it settled into the curved V shape of two touching containers, which started spinning the jar as well. It got carried along, bouncing and flipping in that angle, until it made its way back to Cleo. She snagged it before it went past, and looked inside.

"It's a beetshake . . . ," she sighed. "But at least it's not cracked."

She tucked the jar and tablet back into her bag and pulled herself up. Sitting on the edge, Cleo swung her legs over, her feet dipping down to touch lightly at the cylinders. They seemed to hold firm, even when she put more of her weight on them. Yorick glided out over the cylinders, almost as if to encourage her. Even then, she wasn't sure she could actually go through with such a dangerous plan.

The sudden arrival of a transport drone behind her made the choice for her.

With a yelp, Cleo jumped forward, the back prongs of the docking transport just missing her head. Her feet landed on a cylinder, and her arms whipped around like she was performing a wild dance. After a few moments, she found that she was able to stay upright by walking backward at the same rate that the cylinder moved forward. Arms out, eyes down at her feet, she found her balance, and she smiled.

Then she laughed.

Then the claw knocked her on her backside.

Cleo had barely managed to swing her pack around to avoid landing on it. She tried to sit up, but putting her hands down caused the cylinders to pinch her fingers painfully, and it was all she could do to keep them from ripping her shirt or catching her hair. Round and round she went on her back, riding along like a potato on a conveyor belt.

"A . . . little . . . help . . . here?" Cleo called to Yorick, her voice chopped into a thousand staccato sounds by the vibrating cylinders beneath her. The skull responded by hovering down to land on her stomach.

"P . . . er . . . fect . . . ," Cleo growled.

On the next cycle, she was forced to roll to the side to avoid the claw. Yorick clattered along the tops of the containers before rising, the skull twisted awkwardly on his little body. When Cleo rolled back, she found that the claw was still there, struggling to pick up the cylinder directly beneath her. She was shocked to see it so close, and it almost paralyzed her.

Almost.

Just as it began rising, Cleo hugged it, wrapping her arms around the skinny part of the arm right above the claw itself. With a stomach-turning lurch, she found herself lifted in the air. From somewhere up above her, a grinding screech erupted, and the claw froze.

"Uh-oh . . . ," Cleo muttered.

They stayed that way, poised just a few feet off the spinning floor as the claw shuddered and hissed. Then it opened abruptly, dropping the cylinder. Free of its weight, the claw jerked upward, forcing Cleo to hold on all the tighter. She closed her eyes when it sped toward the slot in the far wall; she thought for sure they were about to ram it. But the claw stopped, and a sequence of lights flashed. Cleo opened her eyes only long enough to see the last few: red-yellow-orange.

Then the slot spit out a basket of peaches.

With no cylinder to receive them, the peaches plummeted to the moving floor below. Instantly, the cylinders caught them, and they started rolling along, bouncing and bumping off one another. Cleo winced.

She had just ruined someone's breakfast.

Before she could whisper an apology, the claw swiveled around. It thrust forward at a hollow, where a charging transport drone waited for a cylinder to deliver.

It didn't get one.

The claw seemed satisfied, though, and it dove, carrying Cleo with it. It paused just above the cylinders, but it didn't grab one. Instead, it waited a few seconds—Cleo could have stuck her hand down and snagged a badly bruised peach—before lifting her toward the slots again. With a grimace, Cleo realized what was going on. Just like the picker drone had taken off once she clung to its net, the claw thought her weight meant it had retrieved a cylinder. Again, the slot flashed six colors—red, yellow, red, green, red, blue—and opened. This time, a dozen bottles of shampoo tumbled out, shooting past the individual talons of the claw to follow the path of the peaches. They hit the rolling cylinders and ruptured, painting most of the containers in citrus-scented slipperiness.

All told, Cleo watched five heads of lettuce, a bag of socks, three blue boxes of flour, and a watermelon sail out of the slot. That last one landed with spectacular effect, exploding with a crunch that sent chills down Cleo's spine. After each failure, the claw tried to deliver its nonexistent cylinder to a transport drone, and each time, Cleo had to endure being whipped back and forth between the walls.

Just as she felt her sweaty palms starting to slip, the slot registered the color she was waiting for: a violet in the first position. She gasped, every muscle in her body tensing. The rest of the colors blinked through, and a build-it-yourself kitchen table kit fired out the slot, but she wasn't paying attention. Instead, her focus was entirely on what came next.

As the table crushed several cylinders below, the claw spun Cleo to a high-up hollow. She waited until the claw had her as close as possible, and then she pushed off, launching herself into the darkness. Cleo landed in the middle of the hollow, boxed in by the four carrying prongs of the charging transport drone. She scrambled to the edge and looked over.

"Yorick!" she called. The little drone seemed to be staring with interest at the stew of stuff churning across the tops of the cylinders. When he noticed Cleo frantically waving her arms above, he lifted himself up to grabbing distance, and she brought him into the hollow. A moment later, two cleansers and a host of repair drones glided in through

several of the lowest charging ports, and they began tending to the mess below. Cleo ducked back into the safety of
the darkness, covering Yorick's lights with her fingers so
that just a little trickled through.

"Okay," she said breathlessly. "That was interesting . . ."

Knowing she needed both hands free for the next
part, she packed Yorick into her backpack, settling him on
top of Ms. VAIN. Then she checked the straps of the bag,
making sure they were snug on her shoulders and across
her waist.

"Fingers crossed," she muttered, and she stepped up to
the transport drone.

Two of its carrying prongs were above her head, and
two were at her feet. A cylinder would fit snugly into the
box described by the prongs. Cleo, though, had to reach up
and to either side, then spread her legs almost triple the
width of her shoulders. She planted a foot on each of
the lower prongs and curled her hands around the uppers.
She was stretched for sure, like a big letter X, and she
made sure she had a good grip before she settled in.

The drone whirred to life, tricked by Cleo's weight into
thinking it had its cargo.

"I've got this . . . I've got this . . . ," she whispered.

And then they took off.

CHAPTER THIRTY-ONE

Cleo wanted to know where they were headed, but it was all she could do to hold on. At least she could see beneath her, and to either side. All around, other drones crowded. To Cleo's amazement, none actually touched, not even when her drone joined the great swirling column of them at the center of the heart.

Not even when they began to rise.

Her failure the first time she'd tried this was fresh in her mind, so much so that her chest hurt. She had to close her eyes to concentrate on keeping her grip and steadying her breathing—the last thing she needed was to start hyperventilating again. When another huge transport drone moved into position above them, its rotors slicing through the air just a few inches above Cleo's curls, she whimpered, crouching as best she could. Her arms began to shake.

It's different this time, she thought. *There's no extra weight on the cylinder. We'll be fine. Just fine.*

Please, let us be fine.

Eventually, the size of the column began to dwindle as drones peeled off to find their destinations. The drone above them drifted away, and Cleo opened one eye just wide enough to see where it was headed. She managed to catch a glimpse of a long hallway, its walls aglow with the light from three green bulbs in the ceiling.

"Two more to go, big guy," she whispered. The drone continued to ascend.

It took its sweet time, pausing in midair on several occasions to let other drones enter or exit the hole. Cleo took these opportunities to twist her sore feet and flex her fingers around the carrying frame. She knew every second she held on was a moment closer to the violet floor, and there was no way she was going to mess it up now.

At least, that was what she told herself.

When they finally crested over the last grating, Cleo nearly leaped off in spite of her caution. Every muscle in her body seemed to want her to fling herself forward, to catch the edge, pull herself up, and sprint under the violet lights until she arrived at Miriam Wendemore-Adisa's shutter. But she resisted, gritting her teeth and holding on so hard that she could see the tendons and veins in her forearms straining. It was good that she did, too—the drone stopped over the hole for several seconds, allowing four other transports to descend before it glided forward. If she had jumped, she likely wouldn't have made it.

Once over the floor, Cleo finally relaxed, letting one burning arm drop to her side. She shook the tingle out of it, then switched arms. The placid drone hummed on, and since it seemed to be going in the direction Cleo needed anyway, she decided to keep riding. With a bit of maneuvering, Cleo was able to swing her backpack around to pull out Yorick and Ms. VAIN. After allowing Yorick to figure out which way was up, she turned on the tablet.

"We're here," Cleo said. "The sixth floor."

"Congratulations, love!" Ms. VAIN replied, and she clapped softly.

Cleo glanced up at the ceiling, where the lights were now violet-yellow-violet. "I can't decide whether violet's my favorite color now, or if I never want to see it again," she muttered.

Ms. VAIN smiled. "I take it we're progressing down a hallway?"

Cleo started to turn the tablet around so Ms. VAIN could see, but then she remembered. "Oh! Sorry! I forgot you don't have a camera. Yes. We're still riding the drone that got us up here. It's headed toward—"

Before she could finish, the drone lurched to a stop. Cleo's grip broke, and she nearly dropped the tablet. It took her several seconds of wobbling and flailing to steady herself. When she had collected her wits, she saw that the drone had come to rest in the middle of the hall, blocking a quiet procession of drones behind them. Cleo strained to see what might have stopped them, and the drone obliged by pivoting to the right, so that it blocked the hallway completely.

There had been nothing ahead of them.

"What are we doing?" she wondered.

The answer came just moments later.

The bulky drone began to back up. Cleo twisted her head to try to see; she was afraid they were going to slam into the wall. But the heavy transport proved surprisingly precise, and its four prongs came to rest against the wall with only the softest bump. Four clicks echoed through the hall, and then Cleo gasped.

The back of the drone's head—the plain gray panel she'd been staring at for the entire ride—began to move. It extended toward her, a piston of metal that forced her to drop to her feet on the grating and retreat to the wall. It wasn't quick, but it was unrelenting, and Cleo had to nimbly dodge out of the framework of the drone. As she did, she saw what was happening.

Behind her was a shutter, its colors blinking violet-yellow-violet-blue-blue-orange. As the drone's piston inched toward it, the shutter slid open.

Even without a cylinder, the drone was trying to make its delivery.

Or, more to the point, it was trying to deliver Cleo.

"Is that our new table, Livina?" Cleo heard. Goose bumps tickled all along her arms.

The voice had come from inside the unit.

Before she could think of what to do, Yorick buzzed in front of her. The skull floated into the space left by the retracting piston, its eye lights shining in through the opening. The transport drone disengaged from the wall and pulled away, though the shutter remained open.

It had to, since Yorick was sitting in it.

"What in the world . . . ," a woman said.

Then the shutter shook with screams.

"Oh no!" Cleo cried, and she jumped at the opening. Just past Yorick's head, she saw a trembling woman. She pointed a kitchen knife straight at Yorick.

He smiled.

Cleo reached in, wrenching Yorick from the poor family's tube. She replaced his bony face with her own. The woman screamed again. A man, shirtless and with shaving cream slathered across his face, burst in and demanded to know what was wrong. He followed the line indicated by the tip of his wife's knife, saw Cleo's face, and promptly screamed, too.

"Sorry!" Cleo said. "You . . . um . . . you might want to reorder your table!"

Then she hurriedly slammed the shutter closed. More muffled screams followed Cleo as she hustled down the hall.

"Adventure, dear?" Ms. VAIN asked once they had reached a quiet corner.

"I think we might have just scarred a couple of people for life."

"We could review proper medical procedure to treat scarring, if you'd like."

Cleo winced. "I, um, don't think they've invented an ointment for what we just did . . ."

Ms. VAIN nodded knowingly. "Ah. You're speaking metaphorically."

"I hope so," Cleo murmured, and she wiped a sleeve across her brow.

Cleo stayed to the middle of the hallways after that, and whenever she spotted a transport drone making a delivery, she waited well back of it. Still, for all her caution, she couldn't help but quicken her pace as she got closer to Miriam Wendemore-Adisa's unit. The soft brush of her slippers along the grating became a regular beat, then a drumroll, and then a clangorous thunder as she sprinted along a passage doused in violet-yellow-red light. She dodged a transport, ducked a flock of repair drones, turned a sharp corner, and then stopped.

She had found it.

Outwardly, it looked no different than any of the other shutters. But it felt magnetic to Cleo, and she couldn't take her eyes off that final blue light. Neither could Yorick, apparently. He flew right up to the hatch, hovering there and beaming proudly.

And then it opened, and he flew in.

"Not again!" Cleo groaned, and she dove for him. But he was already past her reach, and inside the darkness of the apartment, she could see him rising through the opening in the top of the delivery tube. She tried to scramble in after him, but her backpack caught on the wall, leaving her stuck halfway in and halfway out. Worse, Yorick's lights flickered off, and she was forced to squint into the gloom.

It was only then that she realized she had made it past Miriam Wendemore-Adisa's shutter . . .

. . . One that had opened on its own, without a transport drone.

The room beyond suddenly burst with light, and Cleo had to cover her eyes. Panicked, she jerked herself free of the shutter, which closed with a bang. She backed away, panting raggedly.

The shutter opened again.

From inside, she heard a soft, silvery voice.

"Come in, Cleo," it said. "We have much to discuss."

CHAPTER THIRTY-TWO

Cleo found herself in a kitchen much like her own. The tube wasn't painted as a garden box, but everything else was similar—the shelves, the stovetop, the refrigerator, and the door, outlined in orange light. All smooth. All clean. The sink was identical, too . . .

Right down to the mug perched near its edge.

A surgical drone hovered in front of her, but Cleo peered past, distracted by the unblinking eye etched into the blue ceramic of the mug. "Why is there—" she began, but that delicate voice cut her off, emanating from the drone itself.

"Just hold still a moment, Cleo. Need to run a few more tests."

"Where did my skull go? How do you know my name? Where is Miriam Wendemore-Adisa? And who are you? Did you know I was coming? Why can't—"

"Patience. I'll answer all your questions once I'm able."

The surgical drone slid forward, the instruments dangling beneath its body spreading wide. They reminded her of the legs on the bug that had bitten her outside. And when an arm with a tiny needle darted forward to prick her palm, she decided the comparison was more than justified.

"Please," she said, rubbing at her hand. "I need to see Miriam Wendemore-Adisa. Is she here?"

"A few more seconds," the drone replied.

Cleo felt as though she was about to burst out of her own skin. Her hands were shaking, and the room seemed . . . tight? The feeling startled her, and it made her think of Paige. She started pacing.

As the drone processed the little drop of blood it had taken, Cleo wandered over to the counter and picked up the mug. It was empty, but it smelled strongly of coffee. She wrinkled her nose.

She had been expecting hibiscus.

"There. All done. It seems that, despite your ordeal, you've come through without any significant infections. At least, none that my drone can detect. If you'll please follow it into the next room . . . I should very much like to meet you."

The light around the door to Cleo's right flashed from orange to green, and a quiet *click* indicated that it was unlocked. The surgical drone retreated into the corner, allowing Cleo to move forward. She took a deep breath, adjusted the straps of her backpack, and went through.

A woman sat in a motorized wheelchair at the center

of the living room. The deep brown of her skin was a sharp contrast to the white and gray waves of her hair, which fell loose and thick about her shoulders. Her hands were folded above a plum-colored quilt that covered her legs down to her ankles. A slender tube, its needled end concealed by tape, ran from the back of her left hand up to a medicine dispenser attached to the frame of her chair.

Cleo's eyes widened. In the dispenser was a blue sphere.

"Are you . . . ," Cleo started to whisper, but her voice caught in her throat.

The woman smiled. "Miriam Wendemore-Adisa. Head of the Surgical Council." She lifted a hand and waved it toward the wall on her left. A window popped up, projected from the lens on the ceiling. At the center, just above a password log-in prompt, was the eye logo. "I'm also your mother's boss, and an ardent admirer of yours."

Cleo's brow furrowed. "I . . . I don't understand . . . ," she muttered. And before Miriam could respond, Cleo knelt on the floor, pulling her old backpack around and unzipping the top. She fished out the can that Angie had used to stow the last of the calotexina and eased the lid off, then inverted it to allow the medicine to roll into her palm.

"I came to give you this," she said, holding it up.

Miriam slid a hand over the arm of her chair, and it rolled forward silently. With long, nimble fingers, she plucked the orb from Cleo's grasp. Then she brought it to her breast and held it there.

"Bless you, Cleo," she whispered. Cleo inched back,

bringing her knees to her chin. Her eyes flitted again to Miriam's medicine dispenser. The woman followed her gaze and sighed.

"I fear I have a great deal of explaining to do, and no easy way to start," Miriam said. "But I guess the truth is as good a place as any. You weren't supposed to come here, child."

"How . . . how else could I deliver your medicine?" Cleo replied, her hands trembling as she held herself. It tugged at the bandages around her waist, but she didn't let go.

"It's not my medicine," Miriam said, reaching up to rub gently at her cheek. "Or rather, it *is*, but not for me to take. I have plenty to last me. No, this was meant as part of your test."

Cleo felt her chest tighten. "My test?"

Miriam exhaled softly. Tears had formed at the corners of her eyes, and she brought up a bit of the quilt to dab at them.

"Yes, Cleo. Your test. Compassion is the first and most important part of our mission, but it's also the hardest to discern in others. That's why we start each test with a problem . . ."

Cleo's face twisted. Tears flowed freely down her cheeks now, too.

"We want to see how you react to having a specific patient to care for. The medicine," Miriam said, and she held up the sphere. "It's meant to get you thinking, to give a candidate a pathology to research. On the test . . . well, in the first hour, the questions are usually about how you'd approach a patient who needed this. You're expected to use your VAIN to look into it; I suppose it was a bit of vanity on my part, using my own profile to form the questions. Still, those who answer them are deemed to have the requisite concern for a patient's needs. You were never meant to . . . well, to *be* here."

"I *am*, though."

"I know, sweetheart. And that's on us. In all our years of administering this test, no child has ever"—Miriam paused, glancing upward and shaking her head—"taken your approach. To be honest, we never even conceived of it. People don't leave their apartments."

"I did. I *did!*" Cleo shouted, and she jumped up, the backpack rolling away. "I got out, and I came here, because I thought you needed that medicine! But it was a trick, and it made me leave my home, and my mom and dad!"

"Cleo, we—"

"No!" Cleo cried. A fierce desire to run away, to sprint like Paige had . . . to *escape* . . . seized her, but the walls left no place to go. Still, she backed up as far as she could, until her heels touched the door behind her, its orange glow haloing the wild tangle of her hair. Staring at the woman through that heavy veil, her teeth gritting, Cleo whispered, "Angie was right. I came here for *nothing*."

CHAPTER THIRTY-THREE

Miriam rolled forward, pressing her hand softly against Cleo's arm. Cleo flinched, raking in a deep breath. "Don't touch me."

Miriam pulled away as Cleo sank to the floor. Quietly, she said, "You've every right to be upset. But we will fix this. Your parents and—"

"My parents . . . ," Cleo hissed. "I abandoned them for you. And they don't know where I am, or what I've done, or—"

"Oh, Cleo!" Miriam gasped. "Is that what you think? No, child! They've been with you the whole time!"

Cleo turned her tearstained face to stare at Miriam. "Wh-what?"

"How do you think I found out you were coming? As soon as your mother saw you were gone, and the medicine, too, she figured it out. Contacted me immediately. We've been in touch through the simulator ever since—your mom giving me updates while your dad tracked you with that observation drone."

Cleo's jaw dropped. "Yorick?"

Miriam looked confused. Cleo cast around until she spotted the skull. He had settled on the corner of a desk near the back wall. She scrambled over to him, flipped him over, and guided the little drone out.

"Dad? Daddy?" she whispered.

"Observation drones don't have audio, Cleo. Believe me—we learned that the hard way, trying to follow your journey. And you nearly scared us all to death when we lost the signal. Thought you had destroyed the drone, or . . . or something worse. But when the drone reconnected earlier today, well, I believe I could hear your parents cheering all the way up here."

Cleo clutched the tiny drone to her heart. "Can . . . can I see them?"

Miriam pointed toward her office. "Sim is in there. I feel cruel keeping you out here as long as I have. I bet they're even still logged in; they're as desperate to apologize for everything as I am."

Still holding Yorick, Cleo stared at the door. Every bit of her wanted to rush through it, to charge in and see her mother and father again.

But she hesitated.

A strange, uncomfortable feeling had begun crawling about in her belly.

"Apologize?" Cleo repeated. "My parents . . . they knew?"

Miriam nodded. "From the very beginning."

A shadow settled along Cleo's brow, and she tried to banish it with a deep breath.

It didn't work.

Trembling, she stepped toward the half-open door, her filthy slippers dark against the white of the carpet. Miriam wheeled behind her, the motors of her chair purring. "Go ahead," she said.

Cleo did.

CHAPTER THIRTY-FOUR

Miriam Wendemore-Adisa's office reminded Cleo of a mixture of her mother's and father's. There was a large surgical table. A chair in one corner was home to a stack of scrolls, and in the opposite corner sat the simulator. From within, Cleo could hear voices.

Her parents.

"She's coming!" her father exclaimed, and Cleo realized that he could still see through Yorick. Blushing, she set him down at the edge of the surgical table. Then she pulled back the simulator curtain, closed her eyes, and stepped inside.

Static washed over her in waves, dancing along her arms, smoothing her hair, and prickling down her back. Before she looked, she knew what it was—her parents, reaching out in their simulator to touch the image of the girl who had left. When she opened her eyes, she saw them, too, enveloping her in a frenzy of colors and distorted shapes.

Only when they pulled away could she make out their real forms.

"Cleo, baby . . . you're safe," her mother cried, giggles of joy mingling with her sobs. She continued to caress Cleo's arm, goose bumps forming in the wake of her fingertips.

"We thought we'd lost you!" Mr. Porter exclaimed. He was crying, too. "When the drone's visuals cut off . . ."

"I was outside," Cleo said softly.

"Out . . . ," her father muttered.

". . . side," she finished.

"As in . . ."

Cleo nodded. "There was real grass, Dad. Everywhere."

Mr. Porter gasped and ran a hand over his scalp. "What was it like, honey?"

Cleo looked at her feet. "I threw up in it."

Dr. Porter's eyes went wide. "Are you sick? The flu . . ."

Miriam called from outside the simulator. "She's clear. My drone tested her. No sign of infection."

"So . . . so you're okay? Not injured, or . . . ?"

I'm hurt, Cleo wanted to say. *My back and sides are lacerated, I have over a dozen abrasions on my legs and arms, and I think the supraspinatus muscle in my right shoulder has gone into spasms.*

And I feel numb. Numb all over.

Like I'm the one's who's made of static.

"I'm fine," Cleo mumbled.

Dr. Porter hugged her daughter again. "Thank heavens for that!"

When the sensation of her mother's touch left her arms, Cleo rubbed at them. Her father knelt down next to her.

"Is something else the matter, Cleo?"

Cleo met his gaze, staring so hard she could see the pixels of his irises. "Why did you lie to me?" she whispered.

Mr. Porter winced, and Cleo's mom joined him on the floor. "It was a mistake," she declared solemnly.

"A terrible one," her father added.

"I should have told you Miriam was the head of our council, and that the medicine was part of the test," Dr. Porter continued. "I should have known that you'd want to do more than just research it. I should have stayed up with you and helped you study. I should've—"

"I imagined this," Cleo interrupted, sweeping her hand along her father's and mother's images. "What it would be like to see you and hug you and tell you I was sorry for leaving. I thought about it hundreds of times—when I was in the dark, and when I was lost. But I never . . . I never thought I'd be so . . . so . . ."

"Angry?" Cleo's mom supplied, her voice soft with regret.

Cleo closed her eyes, focusing on the hollowness in her stomach, both empty and heavy all at once. There was no medical diagnosis that could make a person feel this way.

"Yes?" Cleo replied. As she said it, the notion grew in her, a fire banishing the numbness. "Yes! Angry!"

"We get it, Cleo, and—"

"I . . . I want to throw things!" Cleo growled. "And

scream! And be sick, and curl up and die, all at once! How do I believe anything you tell me ever again? How do I stop this? How do I . . ."

"Forgive us?" her father whispered.

"Yes!" Cleo shouted.

He reached out, clasping his hands around hers. The energy of it crackled quietly.

"You let us earn it."

"Please, Cleo?" her mother added. "We'll make this up to you."

Cleo forced herself to look at them, to stare them down. The depth of their worry, the intensity of their love, the clarity of their heartache—none of it wavered. And as she looked, Cleo slowly felt the anger in her dissipate, replaced by confusion and a bone-deep weariness. She wanted to blame them, to punish them. But she also wanted so desperately to fall into her father's arms, to let him pick her up and carry her someplace safe.

Eventually, she let that feeling win.

"I . . . I want to come home," Cleo murmured, digging her fingers into her shoulder, seeking the sore spot. Something still felt . . . *off*? But she added, "Please."

"Of course!" her mother exclaimed.

"Miriam, are you there?" Mr. Porter called.

"Absolutely!"

"Can we ask you to help get our daughter back to us?"

"Whatever she needs."

"Thank you," he replied, and then Cleo was again

enveloped by the ghosts of her mother and father. They stayed that way until the simulators warned them that their power was nearly drained.

"We'll be with you every step of the way," Cleo's mom said.

Mr. Porter nodded. "Just make sure to keep the drone with you."

Cleo managed a smile. "His name is Yorick. And he's very clumsy."

Mr. Porter laughed. "You try watching through his eyes. It gave your mother headaches after just a few minutes . . . and she's been flying surgical drones for ten years!"

"It's quite late," Miriam interjected. "Perhaps Cleo should stay the night? We'll get her on her way first thing tomorrow."

Cleo's parents agreed. Then, after a few more hugs and promises to see each other soon, they logged off. The specter of her mother's touch lingered on Cleo's cheek, right next to the pale tracks of her tears.

CHAPTER THIRTY-FIVE

Curled up on the couch, her wet hair plastered to the pillow, Cleo watched the line of light seeping from beneath Miriam's bedroom door. Even when it dimmed, even after it disappeared, she remained alert, counting the minutes and scratching at the places where she had reapplied antiseptic after her shower. Only when she heard the rattle of the woman's snores did she dare to unfurl the new scroll Miriam had given her. She turned it on, winced at the sudden brightness, and whispered her way into the VAIN system.

"Well!" Ms. VAIN exclaimed, looking about as if her room had been redecorated. "Fancy! And I can see you, Cleo! You look . . . sad?"

"Did you know?" Cleo murmured.

Ms. VAIN adjusted her glasses. "Did I know what, love?"

"The medicine. My test. Miriam. Did you know it was all a lie?"

Ms. VAIN read the tension in Cleo's voice. Then she sighed deeply. "Ah. I see. The medicine was an incentive to motivate your studies."

"It was a *trick*."

Ms. VAIN nodded. "That is a valid interpretation, dear. And no, I had no knowledge of it. The format of the test is not uploaded to the VAIN database, likely to prevent students from accessing the specifics of the exam prior to its administration."

Cleo exhaled softly, feeling the bandages contract as her belly did.

"I don't know if that helps you feel better."

She shrugged, the blankets bunching around her.

"I could tell you a story about adults lying to children?" Ms. VAIN suggested, blinking. "There are 21,791,362 of them in the database."

Cleo's jaw dropped. "That's awful!"

"It may be worth noting that fully fifty-four percent of the adults in the narratives lied to protect the child."

"And the other forty-six percent?" Cleo asked, her eyes narrowing.

Ms. VAIN straightened up at her desk. "A variety of reasons . . . ," she responded.

Cleo peered at her.

"Only four-tenths of a percent of which consist of luring children into ovens to cook and eat them."

"Ms. VAIN!"

"I'm confident that wasn't your parents' motivation!"

"Thanks," Cleo murmured. "Very reassuring."

"And yet, I sense that you're not reassured."

Cleo shook her head. "It's hard to explain. I mean, yeah, I hate that my parents lied to me, and that I didn't help Miriam. But it feels bigger than that, you know?"

"How so?"

"I thought it *was* real. For three days."

"And?"

"And it was the most difficult thing I ever had to do. I was a scarecrow blade or a bad fall away from dying. What if it hadn't been for a lie, but for something really, really important? What if I hadn't made it?"

"No need to worry about that though, love. The building—"

"That's just it!" Cleo insisted. "All of us, crammed in here, trying to protect ourselves from a problem that doesn't exist anymore. What if that means we won't be able to deal with the problems that might be coming? We have no way to stop them. No way to reach each other if something truly bad happens!"

"Truly bad?"

Cleo exhaled, not sure whether she wanted to let herself grapple with everything she was thinking. She knew that if she allowed herself to, there would be room in her brain for little else. But Ms. VAIN was patient, and she was wise.

And she was listening.

Cleo took a deep, trembling breath. Then she began, proceeding as nervously and desperately as she had in those first steps outside her apartment. "Paige's building failed. Her people *died*, Ms. VAIN. What if our building shuts down like hers? Won't it have to, eventually? Angie said the world gets inside. Well, I've seen it—there are rats and mice and doglike things with masks and ringtails and . . ."

"Raccoons?"

"Maybe those, too! They're already here, sneaking into a place that's supposed to be safe! The point is, this building . . . *home* . . . what happens when the problem isn't just a lie, or some calotexina florinase that needs to be delivered? Aren't we . . . aren't we trapped?"

Cleo's voice faltered, and her gaze drifted toward the ceiling. It seemed so close, like it was crushing down on her. Shivering, she cast around for her silky blanket, and when she found it, she pulled it up beneath her chin. Then Cleo returned to the comforting silhouette on her screen. Ms. VAIN held her hands out apologetically.

"I'm sorry, Cleo. I'm not particularly good at speculation."

"It's . . . it's okay," Cleo replied, interrupting herself with a ferocious yawn. "I don't really expect answers. I think I'm kind of asking myself these questions, if that makes sense."

"That's often the most important person to ask."

Cleo nodded, and she nuzzled down into the cushions of the couch. "Maybe . . . maybe I just need some sleep. I've got a big day tomorrow."

"Ah, yes. And your test is the day after that . . ."

Cleo shook her head. "I don't have to take it."

"Oh?"

"Miriam told me. She's granting me access to the level two program. Says what I went through was test enough for her."

"Congratulations, Cleo!" Ms. VAIN said, though her voice became more somber as she spied Cleo's pensive look. "That is, if—given your recent disappointment—you still wish to be a surgeon?"

Cleo smiled wanly. "Absolutely. I may not have helped Miriam, but that's the one thing that still feels right about all this. I think I know what I'm meant to do."

"In that case, I should say that your trip wasn't for naught after all. There's comfort in that, yes? Not the success you were hoping for, but one nonetheless?"

Cleo yawned again. "I guess so. Thanks, Ms. VAIN. And good night."

"Good night, love," Ms. VAIN whispered.

Cleo watched her teacher's image fade, and then she gently rolled her scroll closed. As she tucked it into the backpack propped near her feet, she glanced around at the blank walls of Miriam's living room, glowing a dull orange as they reflected the light of the bedroom door. Then she lay back and closed her eyes. Her questions swirled there, bright as daylight. And as long as they remained, there was no way she could agree that her journey had been a success.

At least, not yet.

CHAPTER THIRTY-SIX

Cleo stared across the breakfast table at Miriam's tube. A bowl of oatmeal sat before her, a mound of fresh raspberries and blackberries slowly sinking below the surface. Her bag was at her feet, all packed with her blanket, the tablet, Yorick, and her new scroll.

"I got to speak to your parents quite a bit these last few days," Miriam said as she put a steaming mug of coffee by her plate of grapes. "They are deeply, deeply proud of you, as they should be."

"Thanks," Cleo murmured, dragging her own cup over until it blocked the eye logo on Miriam's mug. Then she returned her gaze to the tube. Miriam poured a bit of sugar into her coffee, stirring it with a little spoon that clinked against the ceramic. The noise drew Cleo's attention, and she blushed.

"Sorry, I'm just a little . . ."

"Anxious to get home?"

Cleo nodded. "Something like that."

Miriam leaned forward, smoothing her hands across the finely embroidered tablecloth. "I can certainly understand. In fact, I spoke this morning with the other heads of council, and they agreed that, given your clean bill of health from my own personal drone, we could make an exception to allow you a carrier back to your apartment."

"Like the ones that brought my parents there when they got married?"

Miriam grinned. "Precisely like that, Cleo."

Cleo glanced again at the tube. "Actually, if it's okay, I think I'd like to get back on my own."

Miriam's eyes widened.

"It's . . . it's not that I don't appreciate the offer," Cleo continued. "But . . ."

"But you don't quite trust old Miriam after the stunt we pulled. I understand completely."

Cleo bit her lower lip softly and shrugged.

A not-lie.

"So, if you don't mind my asking, how *will* you get home?"

Cleo took a bite of oatmeal, chewing a blackberry while she thought. "I'll probably find an empty transport drone . . . one that can hold my weight. Then I'll hop on, ride it down, and see if I can jump off at the right time. If I miss my floor, I can always make my way to the heart and go from there."

"Unbelievable," Miriam said. "I may be having breakfast with the bravest young woman I've ever met."

Cleo tilted her head. "How many *have* you met?"

Miriam smiled and shook her head. "In person? Just one. But she's very special."

Cleo couldn't help but smile, too. Together, they finished breakfast, and Cleo helped clear the table. Then she took Miriam's hand.

"I'm glad you're safe, even if I didn't have anything to do with it."

Miriam looked up at her, clasping Cleo's hand between hers. "I've no doubt you'll help countless people before you're through, Cleo. For now, though, let *me* help *you*. Tell me. If I can't call a carrier, what else can I do to make your trip home easier? Food? A new pair of slippers?"

Cleo twisted to look into Miriam's living room, at the wall that served as her network screen. "If I could order something, I can use the transport drone to get out. Maybe even to get home, if it's the right size."

Miriam pulled away, spinning her chair so Cleo could get past. "Whatever you like, sweetheart."

"Thank you," Cleo said.

Twenty minutes later, as she and Miriam watched, the shutter at the end of the tube flipped open. A nearly perfect cube, one wrapped in glossy red paper, slid in. Cleo pulled back the hatch and eased it out. Then she opened her backpack, hollowed out space in the middle of her silky blanket, and nestled the box inside.

"You ordered . . . more medicine?" Miriam asked, arching her thick eyebrows.

Cleo nodded. "Methylprednisolone."

"That's an odd choice. Used to treat rheumatoid arthritis, mostly."

"Oh, I know," Cleo said, and she hoisted her backpack into the tube. After shaking Miriam's hand, Cleo climbed in, too.

Then, with a wriggle, a twist, and a heave, the girl was gone.

EPILOGUE

Angie Purnell dozed comfortably in her little chair, chin to chest, her nostrils flaring with every lazy breath. The fire had long since crackled and hissed its way to embers, but the old woman was warm enough. Outside, the wind curled about the house, whipping snowflakes away before they had a chance to stick on the steps. It wasn't their first snowfall of the year, but it promised to be the first of any consequence, so naturally Paige had gone out to play. That meant peace inside, which meant naptime, even if it was Saturday.

Or, as Paige had taken to calling it, Cleo Day.

At the sudden *thump-thump-thump* of boots on the front steps, Angie's left eye opened. It'd take the right another few seconds to join it. The old woman clicked her tongue and sat forward, taking a moment to enjoy the popping of her joints—a sensation that didn't hurt nearly so much these days.

With a sharp screen-door bang and a fierce gust of cold, Paige clomped in. The knit hat she wore was two sizes too big, and she had to take off a mitten to shove the hat up far enough so she could see. When she spotted Angie, she scurried over.

"Angie, Cleo's—"

"Eh! Your feet aren't filthy, are they? I won't have muddy boots on—"

Paige kicked a foot up, bringing it nearly to Angie's eye level. The stretches Cleo had shown her were paying off.

"Nah. See? Just a lil' grungy. But who cares! Cleo's comin'! I saw her on the road!"

"Settle down. She visits every week."

"Not in the snow, though!" Paige squealed, and she hopped up and down. "We're gonna have a snowball fight, 'n' I'm gonna win, on account of Cleo can't throw worth a dang."

Angie reached for her stick and used it to bring herself to a stand. Suddenly feeling the cold Paige had let in, she shivered and prodded at the fire, which responded with a few reluctant sparks.

"Close the door, Paige. Cleo'll be along directly."

"Can't! I'm goin' back out!"

Angie rolled her eyes. "'Course you are. Who needs a guard dog when I've got you?"

Paige smiled a gappy grin—she had lost two more

teeth in November alone, and one of her molars was wiggly. Slipping her hat into place, she said, "Better start the tea!"

Angie sighed, but she enjoyed their little ritual almost as much as the girls.

"Got it. Three cups, comin' right up."

"Better make that five!" Paige shouted, and she shot onto the porch, the door clattering behind her.

Angie paused, blinked a few times, then gasped. She hurried to the window, tugging the curtain aside and peering out into the swirl of snow. Paige sprinted down the hill, up the driveway, and to the road, where she met another girl and her companions—a floating human skull and a stuffed elephant named Elly.

"Five cups," Angie murmured, chuckling and shaking her head. "Ridiculous child."

Before shuffling into the kitchen to put on the pot, the old woman stole one more glance out the window. That far in the distance, the two girls seemed no bigger than pebbles, but they were coming on fast.

ACKNOWLEDGMENTS

When I first sat down to think about this story, I knew I wanted to write a main character driven by fierce compassion, intense curiosity, and a deep need to help people. I imagined each facet of Cleo's personality as essential to being human, as necessary for our survival as a brain or heart or lungs. Now, almost two years after finishing the first draft of Cleo's story, I find myself writing these acknowledgments while news of a real-life pandemic plays in the background. My family, like so many of yours, is sheltering in place, doing our part to slow the spread of a dangerous virus. Days, or perhaps months, or maybe years from now, when we look back on this period of history, I believe we'll see first those stories of real-life Cleos - the doctors and nurses, scientists and teachers, grocery store workers and pharmacists, reporters and sanitation specialists and EMTs and volunteers - who felt, during a scary and unsure time, the call to be compassionate. So, to them, and to every single person out there that sacrificed something or continues to sacrifice to keep the world safe, I thank you. I acknowledge you. I see you, and I'm grateful.

Bringing a book into the world is always a labor of love, and this one was no exception. To do so, I had the help of not one, but two phenomenal agents and friends: Rebecca Stead and Faye Bender. Thank you for your advice, editorial know-how, and enthusiasm for this tiny odyssey. All kudos to my beloved team at Feiwel and Friends, too: Liz Szabla, my kind-hearted and gently-nudging editor, from whom came the poke that led to the thought that grew into Paige; Morgan Rath in publicity, who helped me navigate publishing a book about the aftermath of a pandemic during an actual one; and, of course, Jean and Lucy and Katy and Allison and Cierra and Kristen and everyone else at MacKids, who have done and will do a thousand and one little things to help Cleo's story along the way.

Closer to home, I'd like to thank my intrepid second readers, who were among the first to take Cleo's journey with her: Adam Solomon, Jennifer Shaw, Don Burt, Theodore and Ruthann Gill, the Simon/Huber family, Jennifer Friedman, Jim Adams, and Annette Ellis. My gratitude, too, to the Wallingford Writer's Community, who welcomed me in even though I'm technically from Hamden. To Karen and the team at RJ Julia Booksellers, my indie bookstore besties here in Connecticut, and to every independent bookstore out there that does so much for authors-

every time you press a book into a kid's hands, a faerie gets its wings. To the students of 5X, who constantly remind me how weird, ridiculous, and wonderful kids are. To my absurdly talented friends in the kidlit community, who do so much to elevate each other. To the teachers and librarians who pour every ounce of their passion into spreading the joy of reading, and who inspire the next generation of storytellers. Thank you, from the bottom of my heart, to all of you.

And, to Elizabeth, Lauriann, and Lyra—if Cleo is kind . . . if she is brave . . . if she is clever and trusting and worthy . . . it's because you've shown me what that looks like. I love you.